# AXX GOES SOUTH

# AXX GOES SOUTH

Fred Huber

WALKER AND COMPANY
NEW YORK

First published in the United States of America in 1989
by Walker Publishing Company, Inc.

Published simultaneously in Canada by Thomas Allen & Son
Canada, Limited, Markham, Ontario

Library of Congress Cataloging-in-Publication Data

Huber, Frederic Vincent, 1944–
Axx goes South / Fred Huber.
p.    cm.
ISBN 0-8027-5740-5
I. Title.
PS3558.U237A87    1989
813'.54—dc20            89-8927
CIP

Printed in the United States of America

10  8  6  4  2  1  3  5  7  9

# AXX GOES SOUTH

$\triangledown$

# CHAPTER ONE

Axx could feel the chill seeping into his bones. This was supposed to be springtime in New York, but it was night and wet, and he was in an unmarked car watching a warehouse on the edge of the Hudson River. It felt like winter to him.

Worse, the car smelled like a hot-dog stand.

"Where is Mallory?"

The man sitting next to him ceased masticating his Sabrett's and said, "Nun olock, I hole im."

Brad Axx, detective, New York Police Department, turned and regarded his partner. He had worked with Bernie Ronan for all of four days, during which he had witnessed the consumption of seventeen hot dogs . . . some with mustard, some with relish, some with ketchup, some with sauerkraut, and some, like this one, with all of the above.

Axx had grown up on Stillwell Avenue in Coney Island. He hated hot dogs and everything that went on them.

"Speak English, Bernie. Where the hell is Mallory?"

Ronan was caught in midbite and tried to free himself. As he did the front door of the warehouse rolled up and a truck bearing the name of a rental company eased out with its headlights off.

The backup on this job was Detective William Mallory and partner, who had allegedly been instructed by Bernie Ronan to be at this warehouse by nine o'clock and who had supposedly said, sure, they'd be here. It was 9:26 as the truck stopped and its driver leaned out the window.

Axx recognized him at once.

The man pointed an electronic key at the garage door, which shuddered and then began to slide shut.

Axx reached for the twelve-gauge on the backseat. His heart was in his throat; the familiar buzz was in his ears. He cradled the shotgun.

"Put your hot dog down, Bernie. We're going to hit that truck."

Bernie's mouth fell open. "Buh Mallawee?"

Axx looked at his partner and grimaced. After ten years on the job he deserved better than this. He started the car, threw it into gear, stamped on the accelerator, and Bernie Ronan's hot dog disappeared over his shoulder.

He swallowed hard and screamed at Axx. "What are you *doing*?"

The truck was a hundred yards from the depot gate and moving slowly; Axx was twenty-five behind and barreling. Bernie Ronan was still yelling. Something about an arrest warrant but no search. Something about putting their collective ass in a sling.

"It's my ass!" said Axx. "You just back me up."

They hit a pothole and Ronan's head ricocheted off the roof. He cursed and pulled out a police .38.

That figures, thought Axx. Standard issue all the way.

The truck had its lights on now and was picking up speed. Axx braked hard and skidded to a stop, blocking the open gate, which was the only exit. As he stepped out a bullet made a neat hole in a side window. Somebody was shooting at him from the truck. Trying to ignore this, he pumped the shotgun once and raised it.

From beside him came rapid gunfire. Bernie was blasting away.

Wrong weapon. When elephant hunting, bring an elephant gun.

Axx fired. A load of double-O buckshot big as ball bearings blew through the front of the truck into the engine block. Axx gave it five more. He lowered the shotgun. The truck was now undrivable. It was five yards away when what was left of it ground to a stop, steam gushing from what had formerly been its radiator. The front windshield was shattered. Nobody jumped out and tried to run away, so Bernie started toward the truck.

"Wait."

Axx tossed the shotgun into the car and extracted a Colt .357 Magnum from its shoulder holster. He went to the passenger door, looked up into the cab: no movement. He nodded at the handle, which his partner yanked downward, then pulled. The man who had been slumped against the door toppled out into the dirt. He groaned.

Looking down the barrel of the .357, Axx saw the driver huddled beneath the steering wheel. This man now attempted to leave the premises. Axx snapped one cuff onto a wrist, the other to the steering wheel. On the floor beside a satchel lay a .45 automatic, which Axx discarded. He opened the satchel and removed a plastic bag filled with a white crystalline substance. Bernie peered into the satchel. He emitted a low whistle.

"Now the back," said Axx.

They went to the rear of the truck. The doors were padlocked. Axx lifted the Colt and cocked it.

"For Chrissakes, use the key!"

This came from inside the truck. Bernie fetched the keys from the ignition. When the doors swung open, they looked in at a young man in coveralls sitting with his hands raised on a box stenciled U.S. ARMY. Stacked around him were enough munitions to equip a small army. He peered out at them. "That's it, just two of you?"

Bernie said, "Shut up and get out."

When the man was locked down, Axx said, "Okay, make the call, Bernie."

His partner snorted derisively. "Sure thing, Sheriff." He pushed the prisoner ahead. "Nice shootin', Sheriff."

That was when they heard the sirens. Axx expected to see a pack of blue-and-whites, lights blazing. There were lights all right, but they were magnetics on the roofs of three pea green sedans.

Bernie said, "Well, who the hell are these guys?"

Axx knew—these guys were trouble.

"Hey, you dummy, halt!" Bernie's prisoner was running toward the open gate. "Halt, I said, dammit!"

Bernie wearily withdrew his revolver and bustled off, haunches jiggling like Jell-O. He had just reached the gate when the three sedans ground to a dusty stop and eleven men in business suits jumped out, leveling a variety of weapons at Bernie Ronan.

One of them shouted, "Secret Service, asshole!" Bernie let his gun fall.

It was quiet then and they could all hear it plainly. All twelve of them turned toward the depot yard and the laughter emanating loudly therefrom.

Axx sat on a small wooden chair in front of a large wooden table on which lay a fair-sized suitcase, filled with U.S. currency wrapped in neat packages. On one side of him stood his precinct commander. On the other, a Secret Service district supervisor in charge of something called Operation ZB1.

The Secret Service officer had just finished calling Brad Axx a bad name.

The precinct commander said, "That's it, take off. I want to talk to my man."

"Say, listen—"

"I said go stroke it, fella."

The precinct commander was a foot taller and fifty pounds heavier than the Secret Service officer, who took another moment to glower at Axx. The door pounded shut behind him.

The moment it did, the commander turned on Axx. "They work this case for six months, setting up a buy that is going to happen in twenty minutes, and you blow it on a lousy Philly arrest warrant for stolen property interstate?"

The commander was still standing, hands on hips. Axx sat there looking at the contents of the suitcase. "I didn't have time to get a search. The arrest warrant was outstanding, so I took it. How much money did you say this is, sir?"

"I didn't. How did you know those guns would be in that truck?"

"I didn't. But I trust Walker."

"Who is Walker?"

"A two-time loser I cut loose last year on a pissy little possession charge. I've been squeezing him since. He did me some good turns. He knows if he screws up again on parole, he could go back and do big time. He's reliable."

"Walker didn't screw up. You did."

Axx managed to transfer his attention from the suitcase

to his superior. "We didn't know about the Secret Service deal. They forgot to tell us."

"I know that. They forgot to tell anybody. They could have had first dibs, they're federal. We get our guy after they get him. But they didn't talk to us, they didn't talk to the FBI, they kept it a big secret. Now they can take their money and go home mad. I could care."

It wasn't going to be that easy, of course. The police commissioner would hear about it from Washington. And for the PC, no explanation was a good explanation. The precinct commander stomped around the linoleum floor of the coffee room. Axx lit a cigarette.

"Why didn't you wait and get a search?" said the commander.

"I wait, he's a gone ballerina. I knew what came out of that armory in the Bronx. Two-point-five million in small arms, semis, automatics. Even a few mini-TOEs, armor-piercing stuff."

"Your guy is gonna walk, Axx. No search warrant, no probable cause for action taken by officer. The weapons, the drugs—inadmissible. A prima facie case, going no-where. You telling me you didn't know that? You figure I'm as stupid as I look?"

With grave sincerity, Axx answered, "No, sir."

The precinct commander paused. The next words came slowly. "So your man gets extradited back to Philly on a year-old arrest warrant for pissing in the street."

"Yes, sir."

"And that makes you happy? A guy knocks over an armory and goes free, you think maybe you're in line for a commendation?"

"He had a truck full of military hardware. Now we've got it. So he walks. What's he going to do, sue to reclaim his property? That stuff will never hit the streets. That's all I care about."

"That's all you care about, detective?"

Axx knew he had best forgo speech. What he wanted to say was: "Ten years ago, no. Today . . ."

"You're putting in for a transfer, detective. Is that understood?"

Axx stood up with deliberation. "Sir." He went to the door, opened it, stepped out, eased the door closed—slowly . . . slowly . . . *click*! In this way he was just able to control his anger.

He went to his desk. Bernie rotated his chair and raised a coffee cup to his fat, smirking lips. The bureau chief sidled over.

"Have fun, Axx?"

"Not as much as I'm going to."

"What's that mean?"

Axx pulled a notepad from his back pocket and dropped it into the coffee cup of Bernie Ronan, who screeched. To the bureau chief Axx said, "It means I've got three weeks vacation coming. It means I'm taking it, starting right now."

"You can't walk out of here for three weeks, Axx."

"The commander cleared it . . . for a job well done."

As he left the room his bureau chief used the same name the Secret Service officer had called him. If he heard it one more time today, Brad Axx might begin to get offended.

After all, he was on vacation.

∇

# CHAPTER TWO

HE pushed on through the night, uncaring. He should have been thinking about what had transpired that evening, about his job and his future, but he watched the white lines slide by and let everything else drop away by the side of the road.

A fuzz-buster's green light glowed beneath the dash of his big, boxy, 1961 jet black Lincoln Continental. This was a vehicle that in his opinion shamed anything Cadillac ever put on the road. It was also a convertible. He wanted to go where he could put the top down.

South.

Which was why he was on this thoroughfare, I-95.

It was the same route the old man took whenever he closed the fruit store on Neptune Avenue, packed them all in the family Ford, and drove . . . south. He always acted like he didn't know exactly where he would end up. His son liked that. His daughter did not. His wife was happy so long as they got out of Brooklyn and she didn't have to read any maps.

At dawn Axx was cruising along a red, heavy-flowing river. Ahead was a diner with trucks clustered about it, a sure sign of good, cheap food.

The truckers all sat in booths. He felt foreign in this place, like a citizen in a precinct house. He took a seat at the counter and ordered hash and eggs. The hash tasted like wet cardboard. What was the country coming to?

He bought a dozen donuts. He would eat one every hour. In two hundred miles the box was empty.

Eighteen hours out of New York he came upon a large illuminated display festooned with flowers: WELCOME TO FLORIDA.

At Jacksonville there was a fork in the road. Left was the east coast and Miami . . . the Bronx South. He swung right. Soon he was sorry. He was motoring through small towns with too many traffic lights and making no time. Then came I-75. He took this and once again was ripping, but there was a price to pay: up popped a procession of billboards that made him want to start throwing donuts, but there weren't any.

He passed an overhead sign for someplace called Kingston, ignored this and others until he found himself and his car drifting. He was into hour twenty-four behind the wheel. Another sign appeared: GULF SHORES, 2 MILES.

Within two miles he'd constructed a sunny, sandy image of Gulf Shores and decided he liked it. He took the turnoff west. He'd drive until he saw water, which he figured would be the Gulf, as advertised. He glimpsed a shimmery surface that disappeared behind a large old white house, identified as BOOMER'S BAR & GRILL. The lights were still on. He was almost past when he leaned hard right.

He could use a drink, and he could use something from the grill.

When he tried to get out of the car, his body insisted on remaining seated. He pulled himself more or less upright.

There was a lot of noise in the air. In Manhattan he lived on the twenty-fifth floor of a city-owned building among many city-owned buildings on Tenth Avenue in the West Thirties. When you opened a window at night, you heard a distant, mechanical drone. You heard nothing like this. This sounded as if the entire insect population of Gulf Shores had turned out to say hello. The sound helped him uncoil. He pushed at a screen door and went inside and the racket diminished only slightly.

He passed among empty tables on which chairs were set upside down. Only one table was working: a blonde and a man in a dark suit. Axx headed toward the bar at the rear. Above it hung a fishing net into which various former residents of the sea had been dumped. The bartender stood with his back to the bar. He wasn't tall, but he was wide. He resembled a large box dumped on the floor.

Axx crawled onto a stool and waited. When nothing happened, he said, "How about a scotch and water and some ham and eggs? Hold the grits."

The man had been reading some mail. The face that now turned and lifted to greet Axx looked as if it never intended to greet anybody ever again. It was etched by the years and framed by a mass of flowing yellow hair obviously stolen from its rightful owner. The voice that came out was a good fit: deep and resonant, but not as harsh as Axx expected. "What we have here now is dinner. What you are talking about is breakfast. Breakfast is tomorrow." He looked Axx in the eye. "Tomorrow check the hardware."

Axx realized he had not shucked out of his jacket, under which the shoulder holster and .357 were visible. The Browning had been dispensed with early on; yes, always the Browning.

"Private security, Pop."

"Private security, my big butt. Those boys come down in new cars with new broads. Ain't nothin' new about you."

He left and Axx heard him speak to someone in the kitchen, from which soon issued a symphony of hissing, popping, hungry-making sounds. A woman who resembled the bartender in age, dimension, and attitude came out with a plate and a cup of coffee. On the plate was something Axx did not recognize.

"Blackened amberjack," she said gruffly.

Next to that was something that resembled potatoes.

"Hush puppies."

When he was finished, he wanted more of everything—coffee, hush puppies, and especially amberjack. He also took another scotch and water.

Between bites and sips he eyeballed the couple in the bar mirror, particularly the female half. She looked to be in her early thirties with blond hair that shone silvery. She was in a frilly dress that failed to conceal extravagant contours. Her tan made him want to explore its boundaries. The man in the blue suit wore shoes that were black and pointy. He looked like he'd just come up onto Seventh Avenue out of Penn Station. He was as pale as Axx.

Now and then the woman looked into the mirror, at Axx. So did the man, but then quickly away. Her face was all highlights and shadows, while his was round and flat. He did most of the talking, in a nasal, insistent voice. Axx listened to them speak of options, points, and parcels.

Abruptly Seventh Avenue became agitated. He grabbed the woman's arm. She tried to yank it away but he held on tight. She stood, twisting in his grip. Axx turned on his stool and walked over. "Excuse me, but you're interfering with a natural process of mine. It's called digestion."

Seventh Avenue glared at Axx. "Who the hell are you supposed to be?"

"You don't want to find out."

The man looked away, half-grinning. "I don't believe this."

"Believe it."

For a moment there was only the ratcheting noise of the insect night. Then the man threw the woman's arm aside and laughed. "I don't need this." He tossed a few bills on the table and stalked out.

The woman straightened her hair and looked at Axx, green eyes blazing.

Axx said, "You look like you could use a drink. You've had a rough evening."

"I've had worse."

At the bar she wiped the frost from a chilled glass and drew a finger across her forehead. "This weather. Too hot, too early."

"Beats rain and cold."

"That where you come from?"

"The other end of the world, seems like from here. Name is Brad. Brad Axx."

"Kristen McCauley."

"You don't look like a snowbird."

"Local, more or less. Born and raised up in Kingston. Fifty miles north."

"Big-city girl goes small-town?"

"I left a bad marriage in Kingston. Gulf Shores is a good place for that. I'm in real estate here. Good job for after a bad marriage. All you have time for is work."

She crossed her legs and the fabric of her dress followed a hip's swelling curve. The dress was pastel and orangey and left her shoulders bare. She wore a lot of gold, which glowed against caramel skin.

"Where did you say you were from?" she asked.

"Rain and cold. Came down to get warmed up. Seems to be working."

She looked at him appraisingly. "Florida's good for that. Glad you're having fun."

"Didn't say that. Just getting warm so far."

"What's your idea of fun?"

"Looking at property."

"Really . . ."

"Anything you could show me?"

"River Woods is all I've got."

"What's River Woods?"

"New planned community about two miles upriver. Nine hundred acres between the river and De Soto park. I'm the broker, exclusive." She seemed pleased with herself. She finished her drink and grabbed her bag.

"See you again," he said.

"Sure."

"River what?"

"Woods. River Woods . . ."

When he woke the first time, it was almost day. He hadn't dreamed and he wasn't rested. The room, located in a corner above Boomer's Bar & Grill, was a steambath. The windows were closed. He pushed himself out of bed. He'd managed to strip his shirt and shoes off before conking out, but he was still wearing his pants. He opened a window and looked down at the water, which seemed to flow under the house.

He had come to Florida to take a room on a river.

On the far bank, only a hundred feet or so distant, a bird with long, sticklike legs and a long neck flapped its enormous white wings and ponderously lifted off.

Abruptly it accelerated, now sleek and light looking, banked right, and was gone.

He was on a river, but he felt a long way from New York. Objective accomplished.

And then as he slid again into sleep it was there before him: Fort Hamilton Parkway, just a few yards from the A&B grocery store, his wife at his side, six months gone. The enormous man running out of the store, slipping as if on a banana peel, landing heavily where he would feel no pain as Marcia giggled . . . the man, huge bulk packed into a shiny undersized jacket, scrambling toward a car at the curb . . . Axx seeing the gun, understanding now, the barrel leveling, Axx's own weapon out.

Two shots and it was over. His wife lay on the pavement, her dark eyes pleading. The killer, with a bullet in him, crawled into the car, which sped off.

When Axx woke again, it was half-light. He couldn't tell whether it was nearer day or night. He went to the basin in the corner, soaked a towel and put his face into it, then bathed his neck and shoulders.

He checked the date on his watch, and checked it again. He had slept for a night and a day and another night.

The first order of business was breakfast, dished up in the bar by a glum Boomer, which was just fine. Axx was in no mood for chatter.

Next: find the beach. It was at the end of the road and deserted at this hour. He swam naked as the sun came up over Florida.

Back in his room. Now what?

He knew what.

The sign at the turnoff was carved out of a piece of wood that had been stained gray. The letters were red: RIVER WOODS . . . A COMMUNITY IN NATURE. He drove toward a single house set among trees: MODEL & SALES OFFICE.

Axx walked up what he later would learn was a poly-pebble path to the front door, pushed inside, and found himself in a living room. There was no furniture except for a desk by the door. Taking up most of one wall was a color blowup of a photograph of River Woods shot from an airplane. The heading above it read, OUR SITE. On another wall was a collection of smaller pictures showing people playing tennis, people in boats, people at the beach, people walking among trees at sunset. Nobody looked unhappy. The heading over these read, OUR PLAN: MAN AND NATURE TOGETHER.

From a doorway to the rear Kristen walked in. She wore a rust-colored jumpsuit that was cut low, and the expanse to which this invited attention was draped by a gold necklace. She was beaming. At Boomer's she had seemed cool, recessed. Here she was vibrant.

"Hello!" she said. "So you *were* interested."

"Sure was. And I'm already impressed."

In the middle of the room on a glass-enclosed table was a large drawing in blue, green, red, and yellow of The Site. It was divided into three "Phases," a few "Sections," and a lot of "Parcels."

Kristen stepped nearer to both the table and Axx. "I don't think you could find anything in this area that compares."

His eyes were back on her. "Not likely."

She quickly reached for a stainless steel wand, which telescoped out. She pointed to the rectangle that was River Woods. "Ten acres by ninety acres, that's about three and

a half miles long, fronting Lee River and backing up
against De Soto Park." The wand gingerly touched Sections A and B of the green patch marked "Phase One."
"Single family on one acre. One acre. These homes will
*not* be shoehorned into bulldozed half-acre lots with thirty-
foot setbacks. Natural landscaping preserved . . . exteriors
of stucco, masonry, or wood . . . roofs of tile or cedar
shake."

Axx liked the ring of that: cedar shake. Sounded like it
would sell in Brooklyn.

The wand moved on to Sections C and D: villas . . .
town homes . . . duplexes . . . and multifamily units, three
stories over parking. Now and then Axx would interrupt,
such as when he heard, "Zero detached villas," meaning
no yard, all interior. Or, "Twenty-eight-hundred square
feet under air." That is, air-conditioned space excluding
garage and patio.

Mostly, though, he was lifted into the silken web of
words she spun. He luxuriated there. He listened not so
much to what she said as her way of saying it. Her
movements were easy and precise. In her eyes he saw
expectation. He felt his joints grow rubbery, and a sensa-
tion he could not identify flowed from the base of his spine
upward. It was pleasant.

"Would you like to see the site?" she asked.

"Let's go."

A heavy rumble came rolling in from outside. She went
to the window. "It's been summer heat, now it looks like
a summer storm." She turned, flashing that million-dollar
smile. "I'll get into my walkabout shoes and be right with
you." She strode out, her limbs doing interesting things
inside that jumpsuit.

Axx heard the front door open and turned to see a tall,

slope-shouldered man shuffle absently in. He wore a pale pink suit, white shirt with red tie, and red shoes. His hair was white and full, combed back. Axx figured him for midfifties. He carried a handful of envelopes, through which thin fingers hunted. The fingers moved deftly. He glanced at Axx, but his gaze locked on Kristen, who glided up, keys jingling. Her shoes were now beige Reeboks.

"Mail call!" the man said.

Kristen snatched the envelopes from him and tossed them on the desk. She put her arm through his and said, "Come over here. I want you to meet somebody." She led him to Axx. For an instant the man's eyes narrowed, the face hardening. Then a grin spread and the eyes widened and twinkled, the face transformed with welcoming warmth. As an arm was extended the body dipped slightly in practiced deference. This minimized the difference in height, which in Axx's case was not great, but for others would be considerable, making the gesture even more effective.

"Brad, this is Birkett Gamble, president of MFC. This is Mr. Axx, Birkett. He's visiting from a cold and rainy place. He thinks he might like to invest in River Woods. He likes what he sees so far."

Birkett Gamble's grin became a wry smile. "I'm sure he does, my dear. Just where is this cold and rain you escaped from, Mr. Axx?"

"New York City."

"Oh, that's a good place to escape from. I broke out of a town called Toronto. Even colder than New York."

"Now you're U.S. of A."

"Not a citizen, yet. Married one, though. A Floridian, no less."

"Very wise," said Kristen.

"I don't know . . . these Florida women, they're a lot to cope with, Brad." Gamble put his arm around Kristen and squeezed, pale fingers digging into firm brown flesh. "But worth the effort."

Kristen said, "I happen to know Janice is a very lovely woman and as easy to get along with as anybody you'd want to meet."

"These Floridians, they stick together, Brad. Don't forget that."

She wriggled free. "I've got to get back to work and make some money for you."

Gamble laughed, low and throaty. "That's a fine excuse, my dear. I'll accept that excuse from anybody in my employ." He turned to Axx. "Brad, I hope you like the rest of what you see. The west coast of Florida is changing. It's growing, but with younger people, working people like yourself. We're just a hop and a skip from Kingston and all its big-city attractions. But Gulf Shores is natural, untouched." He gestured at the aerial photograph on the wall. "And in River Woods, we're keeping it that way. You came to the right place at the right time. Welcome."

This was delivered with such élan that Axx could not help but feel welcome. Kristen stood next to him—blond, beautiful, waiting.

Axx said, "A pleasure to be here."

"Come on, Brad, before that storm blows in."

The smile on Birkett Gamble's face clicked off. To Kristen he said, "May I speak with you for a moment, my dear?" By its tone, it was a question with a single answer. They went into a side room and closed the door. Muffled voices grew loud.

When Kristen came out, she was grim-faced. She

dropped her keys, fumbled them, and finally forced a laugh. "I think we're ready to leave now."

The van in which potential buyers were motored around River Woods had an ignition problem. "And Annie is using the other one." Kristen twisted the key once again, drawing another sickly whine from under the hood. She rapped the dash.

"Easy does it," said Axx. "We can take my car."

"Fine!"

She walked right past it. "Here." He got in and pushed the passenger door open for her.

"Wow . . . what year is this?"

"The one you were born in."

"Who's selling who?"

She draped one arm out the window, the other along the back of the seat. Like Marcia used to do. Axx fired up all 407 cubic inches and eased toward the road. The engine droned deeply.

"I love it." Her eyes danced.

"Where to?"

"Go left."

He leisurely followed new blacktop into the further reaches of Phase One. Kristen provided a running commentary on the local vegetation: mossy live oaks spreading enormous branches; a stand of beech trees along the river; cabbage palms soaring sixty feet; clumps of palmetto bushes; and pines, slash pines everywhere.

The land was flat and looked limitless. Axx felt himself in some primitive place.

Now and again as she talked she placed a cool hand on his forearm. He wondered if this was part of the pitch. He kept waiting for her to do it again.

"One third of River Woods is going to be left green," she said. "That's three hundred acres. There are five natural lakes, all of which will be preserved, including one of thirty acres for swimming, fishing, and boating—no powerboats, of course."

"By the way," he said, "where does your friend fit into all this?"

"Which friend?"

"Mr. Corporate."

She snickered. "Walter? Oh, he's just comptroller for MFC. He's head bookkeeper, paymaster, and he handles some of the little jobs Birkett can't be bothered with. He's also my escort on company promotions, or when I need to be seen somewhere."

Axx caught a blur of yellowish motion. It stopped sideways in the middle of the road, watching them. It was a cat—a very big cat, with a stub of a tail. Axx hit the brakes and reached into a vinyl bag on the backseat. He slipped the safety on the .357, but the cat had already made tracks.

Kristen was gawking at the gun. He put it back in the bag. "Is that thing legal?" she said.

"I'm a cop."

"Oh."

"Who was that in the road, by the way?"

"Bobcat."

He peered into the underbrush where it had disappeared. "Are there many of those boys around town?"

"A few. This is still wild country."

They drove on. At one turn they approached two men standing by a battered maroon pickup truck. They wore workclothes and hard hats. "Well, what's this?" said Kristen. Axx pulled over and they got out.

"Who are you fellows?" Kristen inquired.

"Road construction, ma'am," said one. He was sinewy, with fine features and long black hair. "Drains and culverts are going in next. Just double-checking the locations." He flourished a roll of what looked like blueprints.

"Drains and culverts? When?"

The man had no answer.

"Next week," said the other, curtly. He bore a scar that curved down the side of his face and along his neck. "They go in next week."

"I've seen this truck out here before, haven't I?"

"Yeah, maybe you have."

"You're supposed to check in at the office. We have to know you're here."

"Sorry, ma'am," said the long-haired one. "We'll do that next time." He smiled obligingly.

"I'll need your names before I go," she said, withdrawing a small notepad from her bag.

"Uh, Bob Watts."

"Frank Garcia," said Scarface.

"You're both with New Era?"

"Right."

Kristen turned toward the car. Axx noticed a swath of white powder alongside the road. "What's this stuff?"

She was kicking it loose from her Reeboks. She didn't respond at once. Then she said, "Residue from the road construction."

Axx looked back at the two men. The white trail ran to where the pickup was parked. The men's work shoes were dusted with it, too.

Kristen guided Axx to a parcel by the water. "Riverfront is prime," she said. A thunderclap sounded and the sky was suddenly black. A few fat drops splashed on the windshield. "Come on," he said, "fast." They got the top up with the usual workout just before the storm erupted. The rain beat over them. They had to move closer to hear each other. Kristen wanted to talk about River Woods. Axx wanted to talk about Kristen.

She relented. "My husband was an attorney in Kingston. I . . . lost a baby. By then Jim didn't want to try again. We split and I went into real estate—residential resales. Ten hours a day, seven days a week. Looking for listings, then looking for buyers for listings. The same ones everybody else in the business is after. Always searching . . . searching. Meanwhile I'm hearing stories about brokers with exclusive rights in big new developments selling twenty million dollars' worth of dirt in six months. I got my broker's license. Then I got lucky."

"River Woods."

"Birkett's done a wonderful job putting it all together. He has a real appreciation for natural beauty."

"I can see that."

"Not that he's exactly a prince to work for."

"I heard some of that."

"He's got a temper. So do I. What the hell, all relationships have their difficult moments." This was meant to chase away doubt, but it lingered. Abruptly she turned up the wattage. The green eyes glowed. "And so what brings a big, bad New York cop to little Gulf Shores?"

"Pure chance. I hit the road and drove until I saw a sign that sounded good."

"Very discriminating."

"It worked."

"You must need a vacation real bad. What did they do, put you on traffic duty for being naughty?"

"I busted a drug deal nobody wanted busted."

An eyebrow raised. "You're a *narc*?"

"I didn't know it at the time. And then it was time to get away for a while."

"Well, Mr. Big City Detective, how do you like sunny, quiet, boring Florida?"

He looked at her. "This part of it, very much."

He was heady from her fragrance in the close confines of the car. The storm crashed about them. They were silent. Bursts of lightning lit her face. She seemed to be waiting. He ended that by reaching for her. The first kiss was tentative, then became searching. Soon they were clawing at each other. The violence outside fed their own. She twisted away and brushed a wisp of hair from her eyes.

"My God, what am I doing? I don't even know you."

He knew what that meant—single man, from New York. "I lost my wife seven months ago. I haven't had a woman since. In New York I didn't want another woman. But here . . . you . . ."

With these words her eyes glinted, then became hooded. She leaned against the door. Her fingers went to the zipper of her jumpsuit. It slid lower, stopped. Her hips began to undulate on the big front seat. Axx reached for the zipper and pulled . . . slowly.

"Now *here* is what I call man and nature together."

She guffawed. They lay drenched from their heat. The storm had let up, but it was still raining.

"Air," she gasped.

He rolled the window down partway. Spray blew in. She lifted a damp, wrinkled lump of rust-colored fabric from the floor. "How am I going to go back to the office?"

"Don't."

He took the jumpsuit and tossed it on the backseat. Soon he was above her again, and this time he felt a yielding of something wound tight for many months.

They spent the rest of the morning by the river. The storm passed, but the sun didn't come out and the land was cooled.

His hand drifted up her back to her neck, then back down. Her flesh was smooth as warm marble.

She asked him how he became a cop.

"I took the advice of another cop, who ran me in more than once. Small stuff, but I was a wild kid. That's how it starts. He told me I should get my butt into the army. I said, 'You have got to be kidding.' He said, 'For you it's in, or up.' "

"Up?"

"The river."

"Oh."

"Vietnam was history. It was peacetime again. The army needed MPs. I couldn't believe my own ears when I heard myself volunteer. When I got out, I needed a job. I went from MP to NYPD."

She asked about his wife, and her killer.

Axx said, "It's murder if you take a life during a class-A felony, which is what armed robbery is. First we have to find him."

"He's still loose?"

"He had some wheels waiting. We checked every hospital in three states. Nobody by that description was treated for a gunshot wound. The car was stolen. No leads."

"If I was a cop, I'd be crazy in a year. I'd quit."

"If you could quit, you wouldn't be crazy."

She was raised on a farm outside Kingston that had a

few cows, a few chickens, and not much else. Her father deserted when she was three. She was raised by an alcoholic mother and an easily enraged stepfather.

"One day I did something he didn't like. I had a puppy. He went and got it and stomped it to death in front of me."

Axx was not sure which appalled him more: what she said, or the careless way she said it. He wanted to take her in his arms and hold her, but he didn't. "I think I may look the guy up. Is he still in Kingston?"

"No. He's dead."

He thought he saw the edges of her mouth turn up.

At noon he took her back to the sales office. The parking spaces were empty except for her sky blue Buick. They would meet for drinks at Boomer's, then dinner at the Palm Bay Club, then . . .

In her office she changed clothes and brushed her hair. She checked the construction calendar. Drains and culverts were scheduled not for next week but next month. She reached for the phone and punched out the number of Birkett Gamble.

She told him about the men working out of an unmarked truck in Section B. "They said they were"— she removed her notebook from her bag—"Bob Watts and Frank Garcia, with New Era."

"Don't worry yourself over construction details, my dear. Just sell River Woods."

"Someone is supposed to call ahead and tell us when outside people are coming in, Birkett. There are two women out here alone."

"I called earlier."

"About this?"

"About tonight."

"I can't make it."

"But we have so much more to talk about."

"I've made other plans."

"I see. With whom, may I ask?"

"You may not."

"I don't imagine it would be overly arduous to find out."

"We'll be at Palm Bay."

"That's supposed to be for business only."

"It is, Birkett. I'm all business. You know that."

"You are making a mistake, Kristen. We *must* discuss this matter of—"

She placed the telephone handset gently back on the hook, flipped her Rolodex to New Era Construction, and penciled in a note. She paused for a moment. Then she checked another listing on her card file and reached for the phone.

The office of the Gulf Shores medical examiner was a squat, stucco building of recent construction. Axx identified himself as a police officer and asked to speak with Mr. Medved.

He was shown into a room lit by overhead fluorescent lamps. The walls were freshly painted and very white. Except for three framed diplomas, they were bare. At a desk in front of the diplomas sat a man in a gray suit who squinted at Axx through thick lenses. "I thought I knew all the officers who—"

Axx stated his business. "I'd like to see your report."

Thomas Medved opened a desk drawer, rooted about, and withdrew a file. "Yes, here she is."

Axx opened the file. The heading read: "Expiration

Report." Stapled to the top left corner was a color Polaroid of the subject. The blond head rested on a slab of steel. Green eyes stared fixedly at nothing.

SUBJECT: Kristen McCauley.

CAUSE OF DEATH: respiratory arrest due to acute intoxication with cocaine.

MANNER: accidental.

She hadn't shown the previous evening. He had called the River Woods office that morning, angry. Now he stared at the page, seeing not words, but an image of her, alive, vibrant.

He looked at the toxicology findings. Blood cocaine: 44 mg/liter. Benzoylecqonine: 44 mg/liter. Urine drug screen: cocaine metabolites detected and confirmed.

"What was the route of administration?"

"Oral."

"Wouldn't you say this is a very high blood level for this type of usage?"

"The drug was extremely potent. We analyzed a quantity not ingested. It was found on the coffee table in her home."

"How much?"

"About six grams."

"What level purity?"

"Ninety-one percent."

That was all Axx needed to hear; he skimmed through the rest of the report. At the bottom of one page he saw: BRAIN WEIGHT, 1,475 GRAMS.

He shut the file. He tried to clear his mind. "I am an officer, but not local. I'd like a copy of this report."

A pause, and then, "The case if officially closed. So it's public information. Be my guest."

He had to go up to Kingston to see her again.

He always made it a point to attend the funeral when he was working a homicide.

He'd come south for a vacation. The vacation was over.

The funeral home was on the outskirts of town. He arrived an hour early. He went to her alone.

Then he stopped at the manager's office and opened his wallet. The result of this was a whispered commentary on each visitor. All were family or local, except one dark-haired woman in her late twenties whom the manager couldn't identify.

Axx followed the woman outside. She went to a tan midsize of recent vintage. On the bumper as she drove away he could see a sticker: RIVER WOODS—NOW OPEN!

∇

# CHAPTER THREE

HE parked next to the tan Chevy. Inside, he spotted the dark-haired woman talking with customers in an office to the rear.

Kristen's office.

The husband began signing papers while the wife wandered about the showroom. She stopped before blowups of villa floor plans mounted on a wall. She was large with child.

Axx said, "You're buying?"

She nodded shyly. "The Granada." She pointed at the floor plan.

"Congratulations."

"Thank you." She shot a worried look toward the office. "Jerry fell in love with it."

"He wants a place of his own—for his family."

She looked down. "His business is seasonal. He sells boats down at Coast Marina. It was a good season, but it was his first. We saved up enough for the down payment, but the monthly is still pretty high. We could stay with my folks another year . . ."

Axx guessed he was hearing an argument known to the

husband. He wanted to say something encouraging. "I'm sure it will work out for the best, for all of you."

She touched her swollen belly. "Thank you." She went inside to join her husband. The saleswoman sealed the deal with a handshake, arm straight out, pumping the man's hand. The wife watched them from the side.

When they had left, Axx became the center of attention. She fixed a big sales smile on her face and came over, perky and wide-eyed. She was shorter than Kristen, and heavier, but not unpleasantly so.

"May I help you?" A nameplate on her blouse read, ANNIE JOHNS—BROKER ASSOCIATE.

He nodded at a metallic three-foot-high acronym dominating a wall. "What is MFC?"

"River Woods is, or was, River Ranch. MFC Corporation is the holding company for River Woods. They took a one-year option to buy about a year ago. It can be renewed for another year contingent upon approval of the owner. He's a rancher who retired . . . to Vermont, of all places."

"MFC is Florida-based?"

"Toronto . . . of all places. They've been active in the commercial market there. This is a new kind of development for them—a planned community on a spacious, unspoiled site, designed for and affordable to working couples."

She looked at him expectantly. He asked, "How much are they?"

"Which?"

"Single family."

She opened a folder bearing the logo of River Woods and removed a piece of paper, which she slid across to him. On it, he read $30,000.

"Sounds reasonable."

"Very, for a one-acre parcel."

"A parcel," said Axx.

"MFC requires ten thousand dollars down. We'll finance the balance through our lending subsidiary. There is no building requirement." She paused. "Which means you don't have to put up a house within a prescribed period of time. That's advantageous to investors. Do you plan to occupy or invest?"

"Invest."

"This is a fine investment. You can expect excellent appreciation as River Woods develops. Do you own property now?"

"No."

"Well, River Woods would be a fine choice for an initial investment. Would you like to see the site?"

"I've seen the site."

"Oh . . ."

"With Kristen."

Her eyes lowered. "I see. I'm afraid Kristen, uh . . ."

"I was at the funeral."

She studied him. "I don't remember seeing you."

"You didn't."

"I don't understand. What do you want?"

"I need to know more about River Woods. And Kristen."

"I already talked with the police. Are you the police?"

"Private investigator."

"Working for . . .?"

"Myself."

"I don't know you."

"Kristen was supposed to have dinner with me that night. She never showed. The next morning she's dead. I want to know how that happened."

"How long did you know her?"

"One day."

"Then why are you so interested?"

"I take things like this personally. It's a problem I have with my profession. I don't like it when somebody kills someone, especially someone I like."

"Killed? The police said it was an overdose of cocaine."

"So they say. How long did you know Kristen?"

She cupped one hand in the other and turned her head away.

"Did you like her?" he asked.

Tears welled. "She was wonderful. So aggressive, so smart, so . . . *good*."

"At selling."

"Kristen hired me. River Woods was starting to move, she said, and she needed help. It was a fabulous opportunity."

"Who owns MFC?"

A door closed behind them. "I do." It was Birkett Gamble. He wore a tangerine-colored suit, matching shoes, and the same crooked grin. "Mr. Axx, isn't it?"

Axx faced him. "We missed you, Mr. Gamble. Up in Kingston."

"I deeply regret not being able to attend," Birkett said to Annie. "I was simply unable to avoid a prior commitment. It had to do with River Woods. Kristen would have understood." He turned to Axx. "She was very dedicated to her work, Mr. Axx. She was a very fine woman. We'll miss her a great deal."

"You didn't sound too happy with her the other day."

A thick eyebrow arched. "I don't think that is any of your concern, sir. Unless, of course, you are acting in some official capacity."

"He said he knew her," Annie put in. Her voice was hard. She was obviously pleased the boss was here. "For one day."

"One day," mused Birkett. "Well, your ability to bond so strong a friendship in so short a time is very admirable, Mr. Axx. Now, if you'll please excuse us, I have a business matter to discuss with Miss Johns."

The girl turned on her heel and walked toward her new office as Birkett followed. He half turned and said toward Axx, "Enjoy the remainder of your stay in Gulf Shores, Mr. Axx."

He ordered a shot and a chaser.

"Can't pour a knock until noon, Brooklyn. That's some bad car you managed to roll down here."

"Runs like a well-oiled machine, Pop, which it is. How'd you figure I was from the county of Kings?"

"Worked with your buddies a few times. Ch-cah-guh, Brooklyn. Came down twenty years ago, just like you— got in the car and drove. Fed up with the force, just like you."

"And how do you know that?"

"People come to Florida when they can't stand it where they are anymore. Or when somebody can't stand them."

The screen door slammed shut. The body in the doorway blocked out the light. It was high and it was wide. It hitched up a Sam Browne belt on which sat a police .38 and started walking toward the bar.

What deposited itself on the stool next to Axx was the chief of police of the township of Gulf Shores. It said so on his shirt sleeve. A big hat slapped down on the bar between them.

"Mr. Boomer, how are you this fine day, sir?"

Axx had expected a down-home drawl. There was a slight turn to the words, but no syrup.

"Keeping my knees loose and my glove oiled," said Boomer. "You never know when they're gonna hit one your way."

The chief emitted what sounded like far-off afternoon thunder. "That Chicago humor . . ." Boomer put a bottle of soda in front of him. The chief drained half of it, smacked his lips. "Leroy Snow," he said, and Axx realized the man was introducing himself. "Chief of police hereabouts."

"Brad Axx . . . visiting in the vicinity."

Another rumbly chuckle, which Axx already disliked.

"Snow . . ." The chief swung his head from side to side so as to communicate disbelief. "A name like that and here I am in the great state of Florida, as far south in this great land as you can get. Never seen a snowflake in my en-tire life. What do you think of that?"

Boomer hovered nearby, fussing with the glassware.

Axx said, "Up on the slopes in Central Park we call that real irony."

The chief paused. "You are from New York, Mr. Axx."

"The great city of New York."

"And you belong to the NYPD."

"That's right."

"Down on va-cation."

Axx said nothing.

"Come down in that big car out there looking for a good time in Flor-i-da. What we call the Sunshine State."

Axx glanced at Boomer, whose countenance told him he was doing the wise thing by keeping his mouth shut at this particular point in time. But Brad Axx was damned if he was going to let another cop, anywhere, bust his chops—and on his vacation, yet. He said, "Why the red-neck cracker routine, Chief?"

Leroy Snow leaned closer. "We had some trouble past with NYPD on va-cation down here. Don't want none again."

"This NYPD is not looking for any."

"Well, you are a city boy who is smart." He emptied the soda bottle and belched. The hat went back on his head. "How long will you be with us in our fine town-ship?"

"I'm open-ended on that, Chief."

"Are you carrying?"

"I didn't retire, I'm off duty."

"You just stay that way. Hear?"

"Looking for a good time, is all."

Chief Snow touched the brim of his hat, small black eyes almost shutting as he put on what was meant as a friendly expression. "Those Chamber of Commerce types who think they're runnin' things around here these days tell me we ain't redneck crackers no mo'. No sir! We are all *Floridians,* now." He flicked his eyes at Boomer. "Evenin'."

As he turned away Axx said, "Kristen McCauley was killed by a dose of cocaine that's as pure as you can get. Ninety-one percent, right off the boat."

The chief paused. "What are you supposed to be telling me, boy?"

"I'm telling you there's no way quality like that hits the street before it's cut at least two more times. Once at the factory, once by the route men. And probably once more by the dealer."

"Why should I give a good goddamn?"

"Somebody fed that stuff to Kristen knowing she was a light user. She took the full bolt and it killed her."

"She killed herself, boy. She sat down in her condo-*minium* villa and she sucked that stuff up until she died."

"Just an accident."

"That's right."

"That's wrong, Chief."

Snow leaned in close now. "You think I ain't seen co-caine before? Big task force down in Miami—local, state, federal, Coast Guard, customs, Boy Scouts, Ladies' Aid . . . They tighten down good. The drug people, they just move north. They like it up here. All that raw coastline, mangroves, and *est*-uaries . . . whooee! Load up the boat, Billy, and bring her on it! I seen plenty of co-caine last year or so. Seen people die from it, and that's just a shame. But I got sixteen sworn personnel in this en-tire depart-ment, and I leave drug chasing to the drug chasers. That big task force, they are working the Gulf now and that is their business."

"What are you supposed to be telling me, Chief?"

"You are all alone down here, NY-PD. Don't get your dick in a whip."

The thud of toe-reinforced police shoes sounded along the wooden floor.

Axx looked at Boomer. "I don't think he likes you."

"You got some mouth on you, Brooklyn."

"Just a friendly conversation between brother law en-forcement officers," said Axx, watching dust billow be-hind the departing police cruiser. "What's the story with Chief Leroy Snow?"

"The story is, that pork chop wouldn't have the job if his daddy didn't have it before him. It took him ten years to get an air-conditioned black-and-white. The biggest day in his career was when they gave him a shotgun mount up front. Before that they locked the shotgun in the trunk and forgot to give him the key."

"He managed to get that patch on his sleeve."

"He's appointed. By a three-man committee. One of them is his wife's father, who owns Dinette City and so is qualified to be a member of the town council. But the chief still figures anybody who wasn't born here doesn't belong here."

"It sounds like you butted heads with him once or twice."

"I had to tell him to go pack sand once or twice." The big hands ceased polishing glassware. "He is right about one thing. Watch your back down here. They take care of their own business, their own way."

"So what else is new? Any different in Ch-cah-guh?"

"Yeah, it is. Up there, they got a few rules about what you can do to a police officer and what you can't. You are part of something bigger than you—the whole damn bureaucracy of police work. Here, nobody gives a rat's ass what happens to a cop." He looked up at a battered clock on the wall. "Open for business." He reached for a bottle and put down a glass.

Axx stubbed out his cigarette. "Later, Pop. I'm working."

Every morning early and each afternoon late, Axx swam in the Gulf—and ran.

Boomer was right. In New York he had backup. Here, it was his show alone—win or lose.

Cigarettes were cutting his wind, so he tossed them in the river.

Now he was tan and hard and he needed only five hours of sleep. He had that fine edge of someone prepared for the job at hand as he watched the woman disappear into a long, low building set off a dirt road. The car she left in the parking lot was not a tan Chevy. It was a silver Mercedes.

A sign over the door advertised this joint as the Panhandle. Inside, a bar ran the length of the room, in the middle of which was a dance floor. The music was canned, the fashion was blue jeans and cowboy hats. He ordered a beer from a bartender in a fancy shirt and a string tie.

Axx wore a pair of gray slacks and a dark blue short-sleeve shirt. He would have felt slightly less at ease in a tux.

To a man next to him camped beneath a hat as wide as his shoulders, Axx said, "What is with this home-on-the-range action? Did Scotty beam me over to Dallas or what?"

Without condescending to look at Axx, the man replied, "Florida produces more beef each and every year than that other state you mentioned. This was cattle country long before you people started coming down in your station wagons and your golf hats."

"I love my cruise control."

Axx was ready to buy him a drink, but Mr. Stetson drained his and bustled angrily away, a five-gallon man in a ten-gallon hat.

On a Saturday night the dance floor was crowded. Axx scanned the mass. He couldn't find her.

When the music ended, the crowd thinned out and he saw her. The coal black hair, which had been worn pulled back at the office, was now full and billowing. Expensive jeans hugged her hips and about her neck and wrists hung gold. Beside her was a man who looked like most of the other men in the bar. Except, while they were large, he was economy size: about six-six, lean and mean. Scraggly blond hair dangled from beneath a cowboy hat that looked like it was the working kind. He put his hand on her hip as they went to a table and joined another couple.

Axx remained at the bar and watched. After a few minutes she saw him. He held her eyes for a moment, then she looked away, defiantly tossing the dark mane. The music began again. She said something to the cowboy and they stood.

Axx put his beer on the bar. The three of them converged at the edge of the dance floor.

"Evening," said Axx.

She stared at him, then started past.

"I need to talk with you."

"No."

"I didn't come to your office because it's dangerous for you. But I need to talk with you, *now*."

The cowboy stepped in. "We got a problem here?" he asked her.

"No problem."

"Nobody asked me," said Axx.

"You got a problem, dude?"

"With the lady, bubba." Axx kept his eyes on Annie, who gazed into the distance.

"My name is Jason, dude."

Axx turned to him. "If I was looking for a little action tonight, Jason, you're not what I had in mind."

"Yeah, well, I'm here."

"I know, and you're taking up space, and I guess I'm going to have to deal with that."

Annie said, "I'd be delighted if you would leave, Mr. Axx. I don't owe you anything."

"You owe Kristen."

The cowboy gave Axx a push. "You didn't get the message, dude."

Axx stood his ground. The cowboy raised his arms for another shove. Axx slid to the side. He gripped the cowboy's left arm at the wrist and above the elbow. Pivoting, he smoothly levered him face down onto the floor. He braced the arm against his leg like a crowbar, and turning the palm up, he leaned forward. The cowboy grunted, but remained in one spot as if he had been superglued to it.

"I am going to let you up," said Axx, "but if I have to put you down again, you won't be able to use this arm until next year."

Axx released his grip. The bartender arrived holding a short club, joined by two hefty would-be bouncers. Not unkindly, the bartender said, "I think you should leave, mister." To the man on the floor, now getting to his knees and rubbing his shoulder, he said, "Jason, you didn't hear what I told you last night, did you?"

Annie was already heading for the front door. Axx caught her as she reached her car. She turned and swung at him—her small fist slapped into his palm and he held it fast. She squirmed, but he held tight until he felt her body relax and yield. She glared at him, wild-eyed. "You're going to ruin it all, you're going to ruin *everything!*"

She stamped across the parking lot into a clearing, across which lay a felled tree. She sat and waited.

"Nice wheels," he said.

"I'm pleased you approve of my car."

"Beats a Chevy hands down. Must have cost a bundle."

"It didn't cost me a cent."

"A present?"

"A perk. The company gave it to me."

"The company. That would be Birkett Gamble, wouldn't it, Annie?"

"That's right. But it's not Annie. It's Anne B. Johns,

Principal Broker, River Woods. And if you think I'm going to help you screw up the best job I will ever have because you dreamed up this crazy idea somebody actually tried to kill Kristen—"

"Talk to me about her. What was happening at River Woods between her and Birkett Gamble and that other sleaze bag, the man in blue."

"Nothing was happening between Kristen and Walter."

"I saw it differently. I watched him manhandle her in a bar, and she locked horns with Birkett at River Woods the day I was there. Was Kristen in trouble?"

She stood up. "That's enough. If you don't leave me alone, I am going to start screaming until the police come." Her arms were straight at her sides. Her jaw jutted.

Quietly he said, "You are going to need me sometime soon, Anne B. Johns. You are going to need help, and there is only going to be me."

She started to shout after him but cut it off. She was still watching as he drove away.

He headed west along a two-lane blacktop with flat ranch land on either side. A cruiser approached, eastbound. The patrolman swung his head sharply toward Axx. In his rearview Axx saw a cloud of dust kick up as the cruiser did a three-sixty. Then he watched it swing in and out of traffic, lights flashing, as it came up to him. Axx pulled over and stopped.

Nothing happened for a couple of minutes. Then the door of the cruiser swung open.

"Good evening, sir. License and registration, please." This was said with what even Axx considered an excessive degree of occupational courtesy.

While the patrolman supposedly waited for the computer in his cruiser to report in, Axx experienced in the first person the power of his profession: this cop had physically stopped the progression of Axx's life. It was his bat, his ball, his game, and there was nothing Axx could do about it.

After a few more minutes he heard a door shut and watched in his side mirror as the patrolman returned.

"We had a report a car like this was stolen. Sorry to inconvenience you, sir."

A thirty-year-old Continental with New York plates?

It might just as well have been Chief Leroy Snow handing him back his license and registration. Let the games begin.

When he got back to Boomer's, a message was waiting for him.

"Graham," said Mrs. Boomer. "Something about Case H-42367."

Axx knew the name. And the case. H for Homicide. Case 42367 . . . Marcia Ellen Axx.

Detective Eddie Graham stood waiting on Flatbush Avenue in front of what had once been one of Brooklyn's finest men's stores. Now racks of clothes from Taiwan, Korea, and other faraway places lined the sidewalk. A glossy enamel sign announcing the presence of Discount Towne had been nailed to a brick front previously occupied by neon script, fragmented shadows of which remained faintly visible.

"We're meeting him in a half hour," said Graham. "Let's grab a cup."

They went to a coffee shop next to the clothes store. Detective Graham ordered a piece of cherry pie with vanilla ice cream.

The waitress looked at Axx. "Just coffee."

"You are making me feel guilty, Brad." Graham opened his jacket, which revealed a widening paunch.

"Looks like the new marriage is working out just fine, Eddie." They had been rookie patrolmen in Harlem a decade earlier. Graham was now a first-year father.

"Her mother could cook, and she learned how to do that at least. Don't talk about washing. I got to stick my own coins in the machine. And that Hoover belongs to *me*."

"Sounds like hard work, Eddie."

"She is the kind of woman who can make a man want to work hard for her." He winked. Seeing the look on Axx's face, he quickly said, "Are you interviewing?"

"Ever hear of a guy named Cain in the twentieth?"

"Killer Cain! I personally knew somebody who got himself out of there in three days."

"I see him this afternoon, Eddie. But to tell you the truth, I can't quite get the scope on what I want."

"Be careful, buddy. You could end up rolling quarters out of parking meters."

It was breezy and cool on the street. "He's a half block down," said Graham. "He's a day man who calls himself Benny Bok. A beat cop named Cheney knows him. Cheney called me yesterday, then I called you." Graham turned into an alley, which they followed to a steel door. He pounded on it several times. When there was no response, he repeated this with greater force. The door was pushed open and they were looking at a man with a thick stubble of beard and shabby, oversized clothes.

"Hello, Benny."

The man nodded at Graham and stepped aside so they could enter. Before he closed the door he looked both ways along the alley. Benny Bok followed the occasional occupation of day man. He swept floors, lugged garbage, and changed kittie litter for local store owners in exchange for a few dollars, soon squandered. By the aroma of Benny Bok, Axx guessed that today's wages were already the property of Avenue Liquors.

"Okay, Benny," said Graham, "this is the man. Tell him what you told me."

The day man scratched the stubble of his face, then examined his fingernails. "Grapevine says Fat Joey over at the pizza place jus' got back from South Carolina. He got a scar on his arm he di'n't have when he left."

Axx said, "How long has he been gone, Benny?"

"Before the holidays. I tell you this because Off'cer Cheney treats me good around the holidays. He always locks me up Thanksgivin' and Christmas so's I can get inside and have a nice turkey dinner. I appreciate that." Axx handed him a twenty. "I didn't ask."

"Take it anyway."

"Do you want to eyeball this guy?" Graham said as they went out to the street.

Axx felt his pulse begin to race. "Take me to him."

Graham peeled off at the door of the pizza joint. Axx walked up to the counter. A huge man in a T-shirt stretched tight over rolls of fat stood facing the oven. He rearranged some pies, removing one. As he turned toward the counter Axx saw a thick scar running from the inside of his left biceps back along the triceps. He was wearing enough gold around his neck to bring Mr. T to his knees. To Axx he said, "Yeah?"

Axx reminded himself to play it by the book.

"That's nice stuff you're wearing. I'd like some of that for myself."

"You can buy it two blocks down at Kaufmann's."

"Kaufmann's is expensive. I'm looking to save a few bucks. How about that one there, can I get a price?"

The man fingered one thick chain fondly. "You got good taste. That's twenty-four K. One hundred for it."

Axx whistled. "How can you afford to let it go for that?"

"I got no overhead. I buy right, I sell right."

"Before I buy I want to know where it came from."

"What are you, a cop?"

"You win first prize. You get the rest of the day off."

The man took one step back, but one only. Axx concentrated on holding the .357 steady. A forefinger begged to squeeze down, just an easy—

Eddie Graham came hustling through the door.

Fat Joey told the authorities he always visited down south over the holidays.

"When did you head north?" asked Detective Graham.

"Couple weeks ago."

"That's a very long holiday."

"I just couldn't face all that cold and snow."

"It stopped snowing in March."

"I was having a good time. They don't hassle people like up here."

"Where did you get that scar?"

"Chopping wood."

"You hit yourself with an ax?"

"A piece of wood shot up and caught me in the arm. A real bad cut."

"Bad enough to leave a scar that big?"

"It got infected. They had to open it up and clean it out. They butchered me."

"Who is they?"

"Doctor."

"What's his name?"

"Don't remember."

Axx did not stick around for further questioning.

At the A&B grocery store on Fort Hamilton Parkway, a man stood behind the register. "I'm the owner. Camille don't work here no more. She quit after the third robbery. We get hit every coupla weeks. She didn't know that, but it didn't take her long to find out."

"Where can I find her?"

"She's over on Bay Ridge Avenue. I give you the address."

Axx guided her into a small room fitted with one-way safety glass. She stood before it, unmoving, while they sent in five men. The ex-grocery clerk carefully looked each of them over before pointing to the man in the middle. "That's him."

"You're certain?" said Axx.

"Positive."

The man was William Woods, employed by the New York Police Department as a crime-scene technician.

Axx thanked her for her cooperation. As she went out of the room a man was led in. He wore a business suit and glasses. He adjusted the glasses as he looked at the lineup.

Then he picked out the man at the far left.

"He's pleading out to manslaughter two."

Sitting across from Axx at the conference table was an assistant district attorney. Axx said, "He killed somebody while committing a class-A felony. That is murder two."

"We don't have the felony. The grocery clerk picked the wrong man."

"You have a witness on the street who made him. It didn't take him ten seconds in the lineup room."

"That's right, but the witness was on the *street*. He wasn't in the store, so he couldn't see the robbery. What he saw was the accused fall down on the sidewalk and a gun pop out of his jacket. Then he saw you exchange shots with the accused. He saw your wife fall. He saw the accused enter a car by the curb and saw the car drive off. There was no felony, there was no intent to kill. That's manslaughter two."

"So instead of life he gets fifteen years, max. Chances are, more like seven."

"Believe me, I'd like to put him away forever. But I just don't have the case."

"In three-to-five he'll be up for parole."

"Yes."

By that time two things would happen: Fat Joey would get smart, and he would get religion. With good behavior, and because he was a changed man, he would also get parole.

The ADA looked at Axx helplessly. He had done all he could. Axx thanked him. Then he remembered: he had an interview in a half an hour. He still had time to make it.

It was a job. And it wasn't NYPD Homicide.

Across a bare wooden desk sat Captain Jeremy Cain, in charge of gambling and vice in the twentieth. Cain sat erect. His eyebrows were black and thick and seemed fixed in a permanently furrowed position, making him appear to be always displeased by what he was looking at. At the moment he was looking at Brad Axx.

"I don't see it," said the captain. "Why do you want to come over here to bust ass for the same money and longer hours?"

"The money doesn't matter that much, the action does—and nobody puts in more hours than me."

"That's what they all say. But around here you can **say** it and mean it."

"Maybe I need a change of scenery."

"You might get different scenery, but the geography stays the same. This is New York City. I hear you're a hard nose. A hard nose in my outfit gets it broken real quick. I see you did some work in gambling over in Brooklyn."

"Three years."

"You've got what, ten years?"

"Ten in."

"So you're vested. I'm not crazy about you crossing over the street—you could put your papers in anytime. But you know and I know that if you want to be here, I've got to take you. You're a hard nose who is getting some pull. So what is it, Axx? You see this as a stepping-off stone, a place to hang your hat, you're passing through, what?"

"I'm looking for a change of employment, Captain."

"I hear other things about you. And I'll tell you this, if you put your mouth in gear, you're gonna find your ass in your hand and you can go peddle it."

Axx had heard enough from Jeremy Cain.

"Captain," he said, rising, "go pack sand."

$\triangledown$

# Chapter Four

SHE called him that night. "It's Annie."

He had scribbled a note with his New York phone number on it and slid it under the door at River Woods before he left.

"What's the matter, Anne?" He liked that name better: he needed her to be in control. He could guess what was coming.

"It's River Woods. Birkett Gamble is—" He hardly recognized her voice.

"Are you ready to talk to me?"

For a moment there was only the hollow *whoosh* of the phone line. "Yes."

"I'm on my way. I'll be in tonight. Where do you live?"

"No! Not here. Tomorrow morning. Eight o'clock. At the stadium."

"Stadium?"

"Lions Field. By the high school."

Then she was gone. An ugly thought: they were using her to set him up. But why bring him back down from New York? How much did he know that could hurt them? The perverse streak that made him a good homicide cop said go down and find out.

This time he flew. He rented a car in Kingston, the only
model available—a Camaro. It was like going from the
*Queen Mary* to the *Miss Budweiser*. He steamed the fifty
miles to Gulf Shores.

The car just naturally found its way to Boomer's. The
big back was behind the bar when he walked in. "What in
the hell do you need in Gulf Shores, Brooklyn?"

"My old room, Pop."

Boomer flipped him the key and eyed him narrowly.
"You sure you know what you're doing?"

"You wait until you're sure, it's too late for the doing."

Axx started to ask where the stadium was, but decided:
trust nobody. This one, he's ex, but is he still a brother?

"Kitchen open?"

"Help yourself."

He made a turkey sandwich and went onto what in New
York is a porch but down in Florida is a lanai. It began to
rain—which is to say, lightning raced across the front of
the lanai and cannons went off on the roof.

He was back in Florida.


"I'm up to my neck in this outfit and I don't know
anything about it. I suppose I didn't want to know at first.
It looked so good."

"Like gold."

"I just grabbed it."

"And now you're not sure what you've got hold of."

Anne B. Johns pulled hard on a cigarette. They were
standing on the fifty-yard line of a football field in the
cool damp air of an early Florida morning.

"Why did you call me?"

"I need to know more about this company, MFC. I
can't rely on anyone in Gulf Shores. Birkett Gamble's only

been here two years, but he knows everything that goes on in this town, and if he doesn't, Walter Ravitt does."

Axx had to adjust his mind to this. In New York you could work like you were alone in a dark room. "What got you so interested in MFC all of a sudden?"

"I'm not getting paid."

"Since when?"

A moment passed. "Two months."

"Two months! Is that what Kristen was fighting with Birkett about?"

"You live on your commissions in this business. We make a sale at River Woods, the commission is seven percent. The buyer finances through MFC Financing, a subsidiary. MFC collects and splits the commission fifty-fifty. We weren't getting our split."

"What if a buyer pays cash?"

"Nobody pays cash in a project still under development. That's part of Birkett's pitch—he'll finance, at very attractive terms. Just about anybody can buy in. Of course, they don't get title. They get a certificate of ownership. When they get ready to build and convert to conventional, they get title."

"When Kristen asked Birkett why you weren't getting your split, what did he say?"

"He gave her a song and dance. Just an oversight, he said, nothing that can't be straightened out. But it didn't get straightened out."

"When he offered you her job, you took it anyway."

"He promised me he'd take care of it. He's very persuasive. Nothing happened, of course. I'm still getting stiffed."

She exhaled deeply, and smoke drifted into the still air. He remembered how she'd looked when he first met her:

a bit player in the production. Now she was principal
broker at River Woods and wore the clothes and the look
of a leading lady, a tough leading lady. He wondered if
her profession turned you that way, or just brought to the
surface a talent you had better possess to succeed. He
wondered if Kristen saw she had the talent.

"What does Walter Ravitt say about all this?"

"He says it's a matter for Birkett. Walter is a pencil
pusher."

"When will River Woods finish up?"

"Build-out is over three years. Phase One is a little more
than one-third sold, which is okay but not great. It'll pick
up when the A-and-D money comes through and we start
construction."

"The A-and-who money?"

"Birkett is going to ask First Gulf for fourteen million
dollars for acquisition and development. About four million is for acquisition, buying the site itself. Birkett paid a
hundred thousand to the rancher when he took the option
last June, two-seventy more six months later. So the
rancher is due the balance. The other ten million is for
construction in Phase One—putting up the single-family
homes, the villas, the duplexes . . ."

"Where did he get the option money?"

"Out of his pocket. Plus he spent another hundred
thousand on roads, the models, architect plans, topo stud-
ies—"

"Translation please."

"Topographical evaluations. Spotting all the existing
trees so they can be preserved. When we say this is a
community in nature, we mean it."

"I'm impressed. When is he going to make the buy?"

"The option expires June first. Birkett could renew for

another year but he doesn't want to. He wants to buy and get River Woods building. He's already filed the A-and-D application with the bank. We don't expect any problems there. The bank is enthusiastic. They should be, they need the business."

"They're in trouble?"

"They belong to a statewide holding company. The holding company increased loss provisions on foreign loans to fifty percent of total loans outstanding. That costs them. They need income. The local branch wants Birkett to let them finance all new sales and construction at a one-percent discount. That's where they'll make their money on the deal. Birkett agreed, of course. To sweeten the pot, he may even sell them outstanding MFC paper on River Woods at a discount."

"Birkett sounds like he knows what he's doing."

"He's got all the ends tied up, neat and clean. It's something to watch him work. I've learned so much in the last few months."

"How did Kristen meet him?"

"She sold a town house to a friend of his wife, Janice. She asked the friend to ask Janice to drop a good word for her. She got the interview, and the job."

"Then she brought you in."

"To work my behind off. So-called investment seminars every other night over half the state. People showing up at the local Ramada Inn for a short course on investment theory—How You Can Make a Fortune in Real Estate!—and then we lock the doors and hit them with the glossy brochure and prospectus and the hard sell."

"Is that kosher?"

"Sure. It's how the game is played. As long as you don't misrepresent what you're selling. And River Woods is just what we say it is. A—"

"—frigging Community in Nature, for crying out loud."

She threw the cigarette to the turf and ground it under her toe. "Well," she said, looking at him, eyes wide. Her voice came down an octave. "Will you help me?"

The talent.

"By any chance, Anne B. Johns, do you happen to have a sales contract with you?"

You want to find out who is what in a corporation, you look at the articles of incorporation. In Florida those are in a place called Tallahassee.

Axx checked a map before he left: he would head straight up 75 through the middle of the state, then hang a left onto Route 10. What he neglected to do was consult the mileage chart, and so found out firsthand how spacious is the Sunshine State.

The phosphate mines along the coast gave way to the horse farms of Ocala and countryside as level as a table. Just beyond Lake City he happily came upon the interchange for Route 10, which took him past Live Oak and across a river that sounded like a famous name— Suwannee.

A gas-station attendant said, "Yeah, that guy could write music, I guess, but he couldn't hardly spell."

Soon he was driving through up-and-down landscape that led him into Tallahassee, which was outright hilly. He followed a wide boulevard toward a gold-domed, capitol-looking building. He parked and went inside. To a guard at the door he said, "Where do I find the secretary of state's office?"

"In the capitol building. This ain't it."

"Looks like it."

"Used to be. Now it's a museum. What you want is the big boy in back."

Axx walked out and looked up. Behind the dome rose a tower familiar in style to any New Yorker—stone and glass and absent of any character. He walked toward it and found himself in the middle of a complex of such structures, all of them new and glittery. This was advertised as the Capitol Center. On a register in the tower lobby he found a listing for the office of the secretary of state. When he got there, he was told he was in the wrong place.

"What you want," said a clerk, "is the division of corporations. That's over on East Gaines."

With this Axx got to see more of Tallahassee. Standing before another clerk, he said, "I'd like a copy of the articles of incorporation for MFC company of Gulf Shores."

"Certainly. That will be five dollars, please."

He found himself pleased to pay it. "When will that be ready?"

"Normally just a half hour."

"Normally?"

"Our computers are down."

Axx checked his watch: 3:45. "What time do you close?"

"Four-thirty."

The clerk disappeared with his paid-for request. Axx took a seat and waited. He was good at waiting, a rare ability with which few are born, but one he had painstakingly developed. If you cannot wait well, you cannot be a cop. For most people, waiting ends with getting on a bus, seeing a doctor, or paying a bill. For a cop, waiting often ends with all hell breaking loose, so a cop works at keeping daydreams to a minimum. Axx watched everything in the office.

A few people entered, were given what they needed, and left. Nobody but Axx had to wait. At 4:15 the office door opened and a stocky man with a belly spilling over his belt entered. He limped badly, dragging his left leg after him. The clerk said, "Hi, Jamie!" Jamie whispered to the clerk as he went by, and she giggled.

At 4:28 the clerk said, "Mr. Axx . . ."

She handed him what identified itself as Form 8, Articles of Incorporation, FS 607.164. "Those are true copies for MFC Incorporated," she said brightly, and then put a sign on the counter that stated, CLOSED.

The incorporation papers showed First Gulf Bank, Gulf Shores, as the registered agent. Under the heading "Board of Directors," Axx read:

> This corporation shall have two directors initially. The number of directors may be either increased or decreased from time to time by an amendment of the bylaws of the corporation in the manner provided by law, but shall never be less than two.

Below this were listed the directors of MFC, Inc.:

> President & Treasurer, Birkett T. Gamble
> Vice-President & Secretary, Janice Kern Gamble

He flipped through the rest of the pages, which included paragraphs entitled "Cumulative Voting, Preemptive Rights, and Limitations on Authority to Mortgage or Pledge Assets." Then he was at the end.

He returned to the first page. Under "Purpose" was typed:

> The purpose is to engage in any activities or business permitted under the laws of the United States and the state of Florida.

Which was to say, anything you can get away with.

It was regarding the corporate activities of MFC that

Brad Axx had come to the state capital. It had been a wasted trip.

There was a heavy thud as something hit the floor.

"Jamie!"

The clerk came rushing out from behind the counter. The man who had limped in earlier was lying on the floor at the door. Another man stood with his hand on a doorknob, looking apologetic.

"Don't just stand there," she said to him, "help me."

They started to get the fallen man to his feet, but Axx saw his eyes roll back in his head. "Ease him back down," he said. "He hit his head when he fell. He's going to black out."

After a few minutes the man was able to rise.

"Where are you parked?"

"Around the corner at Jiffy's."

"He shouldn't go alone," said the clerk.

"I'm parked there," said Axx.

They were out on East Gaines when the man said, "This leg ain't worth a damn."

"When did it go bum?"

"Took a bullet in the knee."

"Nam?"

The man laughed. "I got out of there in one piece. It was San Francisco did this to me. I was a police officer. I'm Jamie Myers. I work part-time in the place we just left."

He staggered, gripping Axx by the shoulder. They were outside a luncheonette. "Let's take a breather," said Axx. When they were seated, he said, "How did you come to Florida from San Francisco?"

"My wife's sister moved here."

"You went out on a disability?"

"You sound like a cop."

"New York."

"On vacation?"

"I was. Now I'm working."

"On what, if you don't mind my asking."

"A friend wanted me to check into a real estate promotion. A place called Gulf Shores."

"Where's that?"

"Below Kingston."

"So you came here to get a copy of the articles of incorporation."

"Right."

"Did they tell you a story?"

"They told me nothing." Axx removed the papers from his pocket.

"That is the point of incorporating in the state of Florida," said Myers.

Axx's eyes drifted over the document. On page two was Birkett Gamble's signature as incorporator, along with that of the registered agent, an official at First Gulf Bank. Axx looked at the date.

"This incorporation took place sixteen months ago. Doesn't a company that incorporates in Florida have to file an annual report a year later?"

"They didn't give you a copy at the office?"

"No."

"Come on," said Myers. "I'll get you one."

"They're closed."

"It only looks that way."

"Take a couple more minutes."

"I feel fine now," he said, "and this is fun."

At the Division of Corporations Myers opened the door with a key and went to a computer console. In a few minutes it printed a one-page copy of Form CR2E036, "Annual Report Required by Secretary of State, Domestic Corporations."

Axx read down the page quickly. "Well, well, what have we here?"

There on line six, under the listing for officers and directors was:

President & Treasurer, Birkett T. Gamble
Vice-President & Secretary, Janice Kern Gamble
Vice-President, Walter F. Ravitt

"This tells me a story," said Axx. "Thanks, Jamie."

"No trouble at all."

"What's your favorite restaurant?"

"Mexican place three blocks down."

"I hope you're hungry because I am buying."

Suite 14 was on the floor of the same number in a high-rise condominium that soared upward on a jut of land where the river met the bay. Axx stood before a door on which was embossed in gold letters: MFC INC. Inside, a girl at a desk was reading a magazine. She had frizzy hair and wore a shiny green dress whose daring design did not mesh with Axx's image of an accountant's office.

She looked Axx up and down. "Can I help you?"

"I'd like to find out. But I'm sorry to say I'm here on business. Mr. Ravitt, please."

"Is he expecting you?"

"I doubt it."

"I wish you had called earlier. I could have set up an appointment."

"I'll call next time, now I know you're here."

"My name is Melanie."

"A pleasure, Melanie. But I need to see Mr. Ravitt now."

"Oh?"

"You out there, Melanie?" This came from an office beyond.

"Every lovely inch of her!" answered Axx.

Melanie smiled and Axx waited. Walter Ravitt appeared. "What can I do for *you*?"

"Brad Axx. I'd like to talk about MFC Incorporated."

"In what capacity?"

"Quart and half-gallon sizes."

Axx walked past Melanie. Ravitt held his ground for a moment, then retreated a step, and another, back into his office. Axx pushed the door shut. Ravitt went around behind his desk but did not sit down. Axx did, in front of it.

"You can't just—"

"Have a seat, Walter. I don't want to strain my neck."

"I'm not an attorney, Mr. Axx, but I doubt your authority as a law enforcement officer extends this far south."

"It does. But today I'm representing my personal financial interests in your corporation. I own one of your buyer certificates."

"In which case I should tell you that certificate holders usually have the courtesy to—"

"I'd like to know why you are not generally known as an officer of this company. When MFC was incorporated sixteen months ago, you were not on the board of directors. When the first annual report was filed a year later, you were. But everybody still thinks you're just the bookkeeper for this outfit."

"Those matters are proprietary, Axx."

"Not if they are part of the public record, and the annual report is very public."

"My election to the board is, the reasons are not."

"I'd also like to know why Kristen was being stiffed on her commissions."

Walter Ravitt's face tightened. "Kristen . . . that little—"

"Not a good idea."

Ravitt licked his lips. On the credenza behind him was a chrome carafe, from which he quickly poured a glass of water. He sipped. Then he faced Axx.

"Look, I'll be straight with you. I'm comptroller here and nothing more. I'm listed as an officer because Birkett wanted it that way."

"Why?"

"He said he—listen, I can't talk here. Birkett is obsessive. I don't know what he's afraid of—that somebody is going to steal River Woods out from under him, maybe. For all I know my office is bugged. Once or twice I was sure of it. We'll have to meet somewhere else."

"Such as?"

"The Surfsider, just down the road. About eight. I'll be at the bar."

"Fine." Axx stood. "I will be very unhappy if you don't show up, Walter. You won't like me when I'm unhappy. I pout."

"Eight o'clock."

When Axx was gone, Walter Ravitt opened a desk drawer and tore a tissue from a box. He mopped perspiration from his face. Melanie appeared at the door. "I said to him he should make an appointment."

"Just get out."

She spun on her heel. He got on the phone. To the voice that answered he said, "I just met a Mr. Brad Axx." He summarized the meeting. "Eight o'clock, I told him. The Surfsider."

He hung up, then pushed a button on the phone. A buzzer sounded outside and after a few moments Melanie ambled in.

"I'm sorry," he said.

"You didn't like that man, did you?" He didn't answer. "That's all right," she said softly.

She went over and closed the door and turned the lock. She eased around the edge of the desk. Fingernails painted purple teased the hairline along his neck and he felt a current race down his spine. "It's going to be all right," she whispered.

He ran a hand over one hip, along the smooth, cool material of her dress. He loved the color green. His hand dipped, then moved higher. She pursed her lips and sucked in air. Her fingertips touched his brow, lightly.

"You're very warm, Walter."

"Yes."

His heart thudded. They would begin now.

Axx checked the clip of the .25 Browning. Full. He jammed it into the receiver.

It was 7:15. He was meeting Walter Ravitt at a location just ten minutes away. He would be early. He would sit in his car and wait and watch and be late. When his man started to leave, Axx would arrive.

He tossed the pistol on the bed. Better cool it for now. Chief Leroy Snow had to know he was back in town. Axx needed to stay in circulation.

He passed Boomer at the bar and went out a side door and down rickety stairs. The rental was parked in a grassy clearing by the river.

They were waiting for him there. At first he saw only the one, easing out of the shadows. He was short with curly blond hair.

"Axx."

Axx felt a pang of regret at leaving the Browning on the bed.

"Some people think you been here too long. They think you should go back to your own playground."

Axx decided to go straight at him. There was a problem with this, though, in the form of the arm that closed down on his throat from behind. By the leverage and force, Axx knew this was a very large man. It wasn't easy, but he could see the first man advancing on him. Curly raised a hand wearing a black glove, which he was tugging for a better fit.

Axx found himself wondering where you bought leather gloves in Florida.

Then he pivoted hard to his left, braced his fist against his palm, and powered his left elbow into the chest of the man choking him. A great amount of air was expelled past his ear and the arm about his neck dropped away.

But too late. The gloved hand caught Axx on the side of the jaw. He dropped to his hands and knees. The first kick was poorly aimed, delivered to his ribs via the fibula bone instead of a shoe. Axx knew the next try would be better. He blocked it and grabbed hold, then twisted the foot until the toes were pointing in the opposite direction. Everything attached was soon at Axx's level.

He struggled up. The punch he had taken gave him a fuzzy view of the proceedings. He looked about for the man who had been choking him. The Hulk found him first. It was a good, clean body block. Axx was now in his least favorite position in altercations of this sort—on the ground with somebody on top of him. This somebody resumed choking him.

He drove a fist into the man's midsection, which brought considerable pain to his fist. But the grip relented for a moment, which allowed Axx to thrust the base of his palm up and into the man's nose. This produced more dramatic results. The Hulk bellowed, blood spurted, and Axx no longer had anyone on top of him.

His mind told him to get to his feet quick as a cat. His body responded like a sick dog, but he was up. At which moment he caught a left chop and a roundhouse right from a figure limping after him. These sent him back against the car. He was certain of one thing: he couldn't take any more shots to the head or he would be dead meat. He saw the next one coming. He deflected it, delivered a straight right, and Curly fell to his knees, then toppled to the side.

Axx now thought he had some breathing room. He really wanted some breathing room. What he got was a two-by-four in its downward arc. He ducked. It caught him across the shoulders, and to his disgust he was on the ground again. He looked up. The two-by-four was aloft. It was being readied for the coup de grace by a man whose face was a mass of red. Axx was acutely aware of his only possible move—a whirling kick at the legs.

Just as he was about to get this under way he heard a sharp crunching sound.

The two-by-four hung against the night sky, then dropped beside him, along with several porcelainlike objects. He noticed another pair of legs. They bent over him. It was Boomer. Axx had just learned the origin of his nickname. The porcelain objects were teeth.

"All right, back off, assholes!"

This was not Boomer's voice. It belonged to Curly, now up on his feet. Sort of. He was bent over, but neither Boomer nor Axx thought about going after him. In his hand showed the snub nose of a .38. He hobbled backward, toward a car in the shadows. The Hulk, whose shoulders seemed fused to his head minus a neck, followed, a bloody hand cupping his mouth. Axx expected them to roar off into the darkness. The engine coughed and died. Somebody cursed. Another try, and the car lurched ahead. It bore no plates. When it reached the road, it spun rubber and was gone.

$\triangledown$

# CHAPTER FIVE

Axx sat propped against pillows. Ice packs were strategically positioned on his person.

"You should have told me, kid," said Boomer. "Every cop needs backup."

"Next time I'll be wearing it."

"What the hell was all that about?"

"Somebody sent me a message, hand-delivered."

"Who?"

"They didn't leave a card. Ever see them before?"

"Nope. But a lot of these home boys would take the job if the money was right."

"They were pros. The guy with the piece waited until the job was blown before he showed it."

"Why the muscle?"

"A small matter involving Kristen. I thought it was a small matter. It's bigger now."

"Kristen?"

Axx explained his view of the toxicology report. "I started digging around MFC. They own River Woods."

"And Birkett Gamble owns MFC."

"You know him?"

"Flew into town a couple a' three years ago from up Canada way."

"The great city of Toronto."

"Married a local woman, Janice Kern. Swept her off her feet in fifteen minutes after every hustler around had tried and failed for fifteen years."

"Filthy rich, is she?"

"Her name means more than money down here."

It occurred to Axx that the bed on which he reclined was in the Gulf Shores township of Kern County.

"Whatever Birkett Gamble was selling," Boomer said, "she was buying. He is smooth as cream cheese."

"And maybe just as slick."

"I thought MFC was strictly Birkett Gamble."

"He might be running it. Somebody else might be funding it. Birkett took an option with the rancher."

"Mud Bud."

"Who?"

"Self-made man, worked that ranch up from nothing."

"Well, good ol' Mud has a hundred thousand dollars Birkett paid him about a year ago, and two-seventy more six months later."

"A nice piece of change."

"Silent partners like to deal in cash. Those are cash numbers."

"Sounds like you spent some time in bunco."

"Not enough action, too much paperwork. But I got a look at how it's done. A lot of high rollers like to play with other people's chips. They can only win. Walter could be fronting for the money man in River Woods."

Boomer started out. Axx said, "Thanks for the backup."

"Like old times in Area One." He lifted his right hand, made a fist, frowned. It was swollen and red.

Boomer's wife, Ellie, arrived with a fresh load of ice packs, big hips lifting and rolling like platforms. She plopped one on Boomer's ham. "Off you go." Then she went to work on Axx.

"You may have missed your calling," he said.

"Shut up and lay still. You are off duty for a while."

Axx woke with a start. The events of the previous evening began to play back in his mind. Boomer & Co. wanted him to take a day off.

Bushwah.

He began to dress. This usually required little thought or effort. Today socks became a project. He figured, what the hell, he was in Florida. They landed in a corner. There was no easy solution for his BVDs. After he managed to insert his body into them, he went to a bureau drawer and removed what is advertised as an athletic supporter. This went over his shorts. Then he fetched the .25 Browning, a weapon that would fit inside a crush-proof cigarette box. It now went neatly between BVDs and jockstrap.

He took the stairs with care, but his eyeballs seemed to rebound off his skull with every step. It was going to be a long, hard day at the office.

And not for Brad Axx alone.

He picked up the pace heading toward the side door. Boomer's hawk eyes spotted him.

"Slick as cream cheese, Brooklyn!"

Melanie's voice came over the speakerphone. "It's Helen at First Gulf."

Walter Ravitt picked up. "Hello, Helen."

"Good morning, Mr. Ravitt. Just calling to confirm. A telex came in late yesterday from Banco Nacional. They are prepared to accept an electronic transfer from us on or about the fifteenth of the month. We'll expedite on further orders from MFC."

Ravitt did not speak at once. Then he said, "Excellent, Helen, thank you."

Helen Angers, responsible for day-to-day handling of MFC's corporate account down at First Gulf, was pleased. MFC was an important account. She was not sure what his pause indicated, however, so she said, "Of course I've already telephoned Mr. Gamble. And I'll be sending a paper copy along to Mr. Gamble and yourself."

Helen was going out of her way, as usual, to provide that extra level of service. She wanted to keep everybody informed and satisfied.

"Thank you, Helen. Good-bye."

Walter Ravitt sat back in his chair and began to review this conversation in his mind. He didn't get far. Brad Axx walked in, shutting the door behind him. Ravitt stood and assumed the stance of a schooled karate expert. He wasn't one. Axx brushed aside a weak thrust. A hand closed about Walter Ravitt's throat and lifted. The comptroller shortly found himself pinned against the wall, where his head knocked against a framed copy of a magazine article on cash-flow management he had written for the American Society of Comptrollers.

Brad Axx spoke in a calm and reasonable voice. "I have a complaint, Walter."

"Garowlpf?"

"I am an investor in the River Woods Community in Nature. I inquire with you about the financial well-being of the parent corporation. You send two goons to break my face. This is poor investor relations."

"Kemmelrop?"

Axx saw that blood was no longer circulating above Walter Ravitt's neck. There was nothing inherently wrong with this, but Axx, too, was feeling some discomfort, so he let go. Gasping and wheezing ensued. Axx went to the wall-to-ceiling window. The Gulf lay below in blue-green magnificence. The comptroller groped for his chair. He turned to the credenza to pour himself a glass of water from the carafe. He loosened his tie. Finally he found words. "I had no idea—"

Axx disliked all claims to ignorance involving incidents that resulted in bodily harm to himself. He whirled from the window.

Ravitt spoke rapidly now. "After you left yesterday I called Birkett. I was scared. I said you were investigating the company and you found out I was listed as an officer. I told him I was meeting you later."

"And what did Birkett say?"

"He told me he'd take care of it. He'd meet with you himself."

"He couldn't make it. He sent a couple of proxies."

The throb in Axx's shoulder had eased. He was ready to resume the earlier method of interrogation. Ravitt scrambled to his feet. "There's no point in this, I'm willing to help you."

"Who is the silent partner in River Woods?"

"*What?* Birkett never discussed anything like that."

"You said you wanted to help. This is not helpful."

"There's nothing more I can tell you, for Chrissakes! This is Birkett's company. I bid subcontracts, pay bills, cut checks."

"Which means you had to know MFC was holding back on sales commissions."

"We're not."

"What?"

"I'm telling you the truth, Axx. And if you're investigating MFC, the former principal broker might be a good place to start."

*"Kristen?"*

Ravitt saw the expression on Axx's face. Now he spoke slowly. "Kristen, Annie . . . and Birkett. Check into who they were selling to. Find out who's been buying into River Woods."

"You tell me, Walter."

"That's not my shop. Birkett is president and treasurer, which puts him in charge of marketing, sales, and financing. His broker was Kristen McCauley."

"Off your track record, Walter, a reasonable man might think you are saying this to get the heat turned down."

"I let Birkett talk me into being listed as an officer of this company. That means I'm liable in any criminal or civil suits against MFC."

"Why did you do it?"

"He said it would look good if I decided to leave MFC. And he increased my salary . . . substantially." He shrugged. "Birkett is a good salesman. I bought. Just like you did. But maybe now I have to watch out for myself."

"Everybody who buys into River Woods gets a certificate of ownership, is that right?"

"Yes, from MFC Financing, of which Birkett is president."

"Is there a list of certificate owners?"

"If there is one, Birkett has it. In his office."

"Where is that?"

"Suite fifteen, across the hall."

"Do you have a key, Walter?"

Ravitt rummaged in his desk, came up with two. "This

one is for downstairs, this is for suite fifteen. I don't have one for Birkett's office. Nobody does but him. There's a file cabinet in there with a lock on it."

Axx pocketed the keys. "Have a nice day, Walter. I'll keep in touch."

In the window were displayed a stereo, a chain saw, a CB, an electric guitar, a water purifier, men's watches, women's watches, and assorted jewelry. What Axx wanted wasn't in the window.

The pawnbroker had the healthy glow of bald men who are very tan up top. "Yes, sir! What can I do for you?"

"Diamond ring."

The man unlocked the showcase and lifted a display of these onto the counter for closer view. Axx looked them over. The pawnbroker waited and, when he saw Axx was not impressed, pointed to the largest, most expensive piece. It was a pinky ring.

"Just in today."

Axx tried it on. "I don't like the setting."

"I'm not a jeweler, pal."

Axx said, "Got any loose stones bouncing around?"

The man put the display back in the case and locked it. "I might have a few." He went into a back room and returned with a bag of purple velvet fitted with a draw-string, which he opened. An assortment of gems spilled onto a felt-covered pad.

Axx made an examination, waved them away. "If I had a good set of works, I could get better stones than these in twenty minutes."

The pawnbroker eyed him closely, then began returning the merchandise to the bag, one by one. "I'm not sure what you are talking about, but I think it is illegal in this state."

"What do I have to do, sign for them?"

"You sign for a firearm."

"There are ways of showing appreciation better than a signature."

The man pulled the drawstring tight. "You may be able to find what you need—for, shall we say, a referral consideration."

"Would thirty dollars be good consideration?"

"It might. Fifty certainly would be."

Axx furnished the fifty. Like every pawnbroker everywhere, the man counted it carefully. "He's a typewriter repairman. Works out of his house."

"Where is that?"

"I don't know. You can find him at the Half Moon, over on Flagler."

"Is he an artist?"

"He was a class-A mechanic until they laid him off over at the Cape. He's got a talent."

"Everybody's got a talent. It's the product I'm buying."

The pawnbroker folded the bills over. Then he gestured to a sign prominently displayed on the cash register: NO REFUNDS.

The Half Moon featured an R&B band whose guitar player needed to either tune his instrument or take it to the establishment Axx had just departed.

The barmaid came up to Axx all bouncy and smiley. When he said, "I'm looking for Harry the mechanic," the bounce and smile faded fast. She motioned toward a corner. At a table sat a small, hunched man in a dark green workshirt and matching pants. He wore glasses and his ears hung from the sides of his head like shutters on a window. In front of him was a Bloody Mary, from which he would take a sip, then munch a stalk of celery.

Axx went to the table. "The guy with three balls sent
me over."

"Typewriter on the fritz?"

"I don't need one in my line of work."

"That's what I do, fix typewriters."

"How's business?"

Harry took another sip and a few more nibbles. "Business is lousy."

"Sorry to hear it."

"Everybody wants a computer—for what they call
processing words. Nobody wants to just type. Even these
storefront outfits, plain old typewriters don't cut it. I get
a call for an IBM Selectric and I begin to feel like I'm
working on an antique. A manual, that *is* an antique."

This was followed by another series of quick bites. Axx
said, "Can I buy you some more celery?"

"It's an expensive way to get my vitamin C."

"It's vitamin D."

"All I know is, I don't feel as good when I don't get my
minimum daily allowance, which is three. This is my
first." He drained the glass and sat waiting. Axx waved to
a waitress, who restocked Harry the mechanic with all the
trimmings.

Axx said, "I need some nice artwork out of metal."

"How many?"

"Three or four pieces."

"I don't have. But I can make. It's one seventy-five. A
hundred up front."

"How do I know I'll get delivery?"

"The broker sent you over? He's a good judge of
character. He must be—he likes *me*." Harry's eyes twinkled and he finished off another stick. "When do you need
the material?"

"Tonight."

"That makes it easy. If you need it tonight, I have to make it tonight. You can trust me because you can come with me. My machinery is in my shop at home."

"Okay."

"Wait outside. I'm driving the blue Dodge in front. Just follow me."

They went along twisting roads deep into the night. Pines and palms were silhouetted against the darkening sky. The pickup pulled into a driveway that seemed to run the length of the county, then finally stopped at the side of a low-slung house. Axx heard barking. When he got out of his car, its source came galumping toward him.

"No!" commanded Harry, and the dog fell in behind as he headed toward the house. "There's only Blackie, and he does as I say."

The interior was furnished in discount Mediterranean fitted with plastic covers. Harry and Blackie went along a corridor to a bedroom converted into a workshop. Harry pointed to the floor and Blackie rested his bones, keeping a suspicious eye on the visitor, who lifted a thin sheet of steel from a workbench.

"That's five-oh, spring-tempered," said Harry. "I have two-five if you want it."

Axx considered what lack of practice had done to his technique and opted for the thicker grade. Harry took the sheet from him, fitted it into a press, and stamped out a thin piece tapering down to four inches. On the workbench was a jeweler's grinding wheel. He flicked a switch and it noisily came to life.

"She's old and weary, but they don't make them like this anymore."

Stubby fingers held the steel to the grinding wheel,

shaping and smoothing until it was slim and trim. Harry put the product in a vise and picked up a small canister about as long as the blade of steel. At the end was a curved nozzle.

He hunted about for a minute or so and finally said, "Got a match?"

Axx fished in a pocket and came up with a matchbook. Harry put on a pair of goggles, then held a lighted match to the nozzle of the canister. A blue flame licked out. Harry held it up. "That will go through quarter-inch plate like it was cardboard."

He applied the flame to the narrow end of the tapered piece until it began to soften. With a file he popped the first of several notches. When these were all in place, he did some more finishing on the jeweler's wheel. He then lifted the steel to the light.

"There . . ."

Some loving touches with an emery cloth and the first of four lock picks was completed. He handed it to Axx, who ran a finger along the edge. It was warm and satiny.

In short order three more picks of varying shapes and sizes were stamped out, ground down, notched, and polished. Axx handed over seventy-five more dollars.

"For twenty minutes' work this is highway robbery."

Harry the mechanic stripped off his goggles. "It takes one to know one."


Suite 15 was casually entered by key. Axx opened the blinds along the front, which brought in some moonlight, then went to the office of Birkett T. Gamble. He removed the means of entry from his back pocket—a leather pouch, inside whose velour-lined interior was a brand-new set of works.

On the office door was a pin-tumbler cylinder lock. Axx pulled a chair up. From the pouch he extracted a tension wrench and a diamond pick. He fitted the tension wrench into the keyway and turned. The tolerance was high; he could hardly budge the plug. Which figured: the building and its parts were relatively new; the locks hadn't yet loosened up. He slipped the pick in past the tension wrench, feeling for the first of five pins that would have to be raised so as to elevate the drivers above the shear line.

Picking a pin tumbler is a lot like shooting a basketball—touch is everything. Axx's touch was rusty. He gently levered the first pin up until he felt resistance. He applied pressure to the tension wrench, trapping the driver. It escaped and fell. He had to begin again, and again. The next time it stayed trapped.

One down, four to go.

He got the second pin, but not the third. He labored on this one a few more minutes before realizing what he was up against: a high-low combination.

Axx was disillusioned. Here we have a luxury high-rise condominium office building located directly on the glamorous Gulf of Mexico, and management installs high-lows because they are too cheap to buy pick-proofs.

Axx slid a hook pick from the glove and went back to work. When the fifth driver was trapped, he was able to rotate the plug, doing likewise to the dead bolt. He was in.

He sat at Birkett's desk, which was open. This indicated nothing of value lay inside, so he went to a four-drawer file cabinet set against a wall. It was locked. It was also old, perhaps moved from another location and repainted to fit the new decor. He went to work on the disk tumbler with a pair of straight wires. It popped open.

In the first drawer were two stacks of papers. Axx lifted the top sheet from one. With the light of a pen flashlight he could see a photocopy of a certificate of ownership, issued to a buyer in River Woods. It looked identical to the one Anne Johns had furnished him as a new purchaser for fifty dollars down: all scrollwork and embellishments, like a bank CD.

A file folder lay on top of the second stack of paper. Inside, Axx found a list of all River Woods certificate holders to date, which was a week old. He counted the names on one page: forty-eight. There were about five-and-a-half pages of names. He went to the desk and examined the list, which was alphabetical. After each name was an address, a social security number, and a certificate number. He ran down the list once, then twice.

He couldn't quite put his finger on what was wrong, but—

From the hallway came a dull metallic clatter. He snapped the penlight off and went to the front door of Suite 15. He eased it open. From the end of the corridor he heard movement.

Time to depart. But first he would make use of the office copy machine. He hit the power button and the thing roared to life like a 747 revving up for takeoff. He wanted to throw a blanket over it. Finally it was ready to do some work. He copied the certificates and the list.

After locking up, he eased along the hallway. Light spilled from around a corner. Cleaning woman? Security guard? Over a door he saw an illuminated sign: EXIT. He took it.

At a table at Boomer's he studied the list. There were 263 names, addresses, social security numbers, and certificate numbers. The certificate numbers had six digits.

First up was Matthew Abel, social security number 157-32-9338, River Woods certificate number, 648-338. Something about these numbers caught his eye. Then he saw it—the last three digits of social security number and certificate number were identical. This was repeated in the listing a few names below, for one William Byers.

He got a pencil from Ellie and went through the list again, making check marks wherever this remarkable happenstance occurred. When he finished, he counted eighty-six of them.

He put the list aside and unfolded the copy of Matthew Abel's certificate of ownership. It bore two signatures. The first he expected: Birkett T. Gamble, President & Treasurer.

The second was in a fine hand over the title "Principal and Licensed Real Estate Broker." It read Kristen C. McCauley.

On his own certificate was the signature of Anne B. Johns . . . and on that of William Byers.

He collected his paperwork and extracted a pack from the machine. In his room he lay in bed, feeling the evening breeze come up and smoking too many cigarettes.

A hundred yards ahead a black clump grew larger. He touched the brakes, slowing. At thirty yards the mass dispersed, parts of it lifting laboriously into the air while a couple just skipped to the side. Buzzards feeding on a dead dog.

He swerved around the carcass. A panel truck bore down on him, horn blaring as it whipped past. He was definitely off the tourist track, in search of the residence of one Matthew Abel, 170 Geddes Lane, township of Ennisville, Kern County, Florida.

He thudded over railroad tracks, beyond which stood a
sign: CONGESTED AREA AHEAD. This turned out to be a
streetlight, a restaurant, a gas station, and a dilapidated
two-story grocery store, in front of which Axx parked. At
sixty miles an hour with the windows wide open he had
not felt the midday heat, but as he stood now before the
gray bleached facade of the store the sun seemed to reach
down for him. Dust hung in the air like a vapor.

In the shade of the porch sat a small boy and girl. The
boy was attaching line to a cane fishing pole while the girl
watched.

"Hello," said Axx. The boy ignored this. The girl
squinted up at him. "I'm looking for Geddes Lane."

On his map the township of Ennisville was an ink drop
with a thin black line through it. The girl shaded her eyes
with a hand.

"Is this Ennisville?" he asked. She nodded.

He tousled her hair and went inside. The store's shelves
were half-empty. A tiny woman stood with arms straight
at her sides behind a wooden counter that rose like a
bunker in front of her. The bones in her chest pushed at
pale skin, thin as parchment.

"Howdy," Axx said.

She more or less smiled. He inquired as to the where-
abouts of Geddes Lane. She glanced away, then said, "Who
you looking after?"

"Mr. Abel."

"Who?"

"Matt Abel. One-seventy Geddes Lane."

"Which?"

"One-seventy."

Axx saw a glint in the hard eyes. "Straight ahead about
a mile. First right."

"Thanks."

He left the alleged congestion of what he took to be downtown Ennisville and continued east. At a corner of the first street on the right was a street sign minus the sign. The road was dirt and pocked. It had seen some rain that morning: gaping holes had become brown pools. In avoiding one of these he almost ran over a duck. One yard was fenced, confining a couple of cows and a horse. The homes were mainly trailers, set on wide lots among sparse pines. In most cases the owners had built on—a couple bedrooms, another bathroom—the extra construction camouflaging the core. In clusters around each residence stood vehicles of many types, in various states—a red sedan up on blocks, a truck listing where a wheel was absent, a brand-new 4 × 4 gleaming in the sun.

Here and there, Axx located a house number: 27, 52, 86, and then . . . a lake. He looked around, as if somebody were hiding 170.

He backtracked until he was in front of a mailbox on which the number "70" was painted in an uneven hand. He went through the gate to the front door. A baby cried from inside. He knocked. A thickly muscled man in a grease-streaked tank top appeared.

"Yeah?"

"I'm looking for Matthew Abel."

The man glowered and pushed the door open. "You with Morton's?"

"What's Morton's?"

"We ain't got your furniture. My sister told you last week, she didn't sign for all that stuff. They already come and took it away." His face was now about three inches from Axx's.

"I think they took Abel with them," said Axx.

"What Abel?"

"Exactly."

Axx turned to leave. A hand grabbed him. This append-
age was rapidly manipulated into a position of great stress,
from which position momentary relief can be obtained by
dropping to the knees.

Axx looked down at his newfound friend and said, "I
am tired of Floridians getting in my face."

The man appeared to be screaming but he made no
sound. Axx eased up. He now heard something that
resembled, "Okay . . . okay . . ."

The man massaged his wrist as Axx went to his car,
where he again consulted the list of River Woods certificate
owners. Next up was Kessler, Arthur. Certificate 224-777,
reportedly residing at 255 Rock Road, Ennisville. Axx
drove back to the grocery store.

The bony-chested woman was still on duty. She looked
at him as if she had never seen him before.

"Phone?" said Axx.

She nodded toward the rear. He found a booth that
should have been shipped to the Smithsonian: fine-grained
wood with a folding glass door and Americana carvings—
hearts with arrows through them and phone numbers that
started with letters instead of digits. Attached to a chain
was a brand-new phone book, a species extinct in New
York City public places. He looked up Kessler, Arthur,
and found him. He plunked a quarter into the phone, also
new, and punched out the number.

"Hello?"

"Mrs. Kessler?"

"Yes."

"May I speak with your husband, please?"

"Who is this?"

"Mr. Williamson at River Woods."

"River who?"

"River Woods. I'm calling about your certificate."

"Certificate?"

"For your plot."

"I already have one, in Fairview, right next to my husband. I don't need another, if that's what your selling."

*Click.*

Axx slowly unfolded the list of certificate owners. He drew a line through "Kessler." There were eighty-four other checks on the list. Sixteen of them were opposite people listed as residents of Ennisville. After another hour in the booth he had crossed off ten more names. For six others the operator had no known phone numbers, listed or unlisted.

He now looked more or less as though he had gone swimming fully clothed. He bought a beer from the skeletal proprietor up front. She gave him change from a wooden drawer. He took the beer out to the porch. The boy and girl were gone. He sat in the shade and drank the beer and watched hawks drift above flat piney landscape.

Then he got in his car and pointed it toward Gulf Shores.

$\triangledown$

# Chapter Six

"WHAT are you doing here? I told you—"

He dropped the stack on her desk.

"It goes like this, Anne—eighty-six of the certificates issued so far at this Community in Nature are three-dollar bills," said Axx. "Eighty have Kristen's name on them, six have yours, for sales after you took over."

"I didn't sign them. My signature is on the plates they print from. I never saw these until now. Where did you get them?"

"Birkett Gamble."

She looked dazed. "Birkett?"

"He was out of his office at the time, which was about midnight."

She fumbled with a pack of cigarettes. Three fell out. She lit one and tried to stuff the other two back in, but couldn't. He reached out and swept them off the desk.

"When are you going to level with me, Anne?"

"What do you mean?"

"You knew about these certificates."

"No! I told you, they were holding back on commissions and I—"

"Walter told me you were paid."

"You believe that worm?"

"On this, yes."

"Well, I suppose there's nothing more I can say."

He gripped her arms. The cigarette went flying. He pushed up both sleeves, exposing her wrists.

"What are you *doing*?"

He spoke softly. "Kristen was a user. Are you a user, Anne B. Johns? Do you shoot, or do you snort, like your ex-boss?"

He found nothing and let go. Her body sagged. "I didn't know about Kristen and drugs, I swear it."

"And the phony certificates?"

She dug out another cigarette and lit it. "Birkett is using them for the A-and-D loan."

"*Bogus* certificates?"

"Birkett needs the A-and-D to get construction under way so we can get sales moving. Most people buy when they see buildings going up. It feels safer. But to get the loan, Birkett has to show at least fifty percent sold in Phase One. In his A-and-D application to the bank, he claimed two hundred and sixty-three sales. We were running maybe one-third sold. So he made up the difference."

"Suppose Birkett wins. They give him the loan. What does he do with the phony certificates?"

"Resells them to real buyers. It's just paper shuffling, and it never leaves the company. It's very clever, really. He could pull it off."

"So why get me involved? Why call me up and get me down here and feed me a story about getting stiffed on commissions?"

"I wanted Birkett to know I wasn't alone, so he wouldn't try it again. He's going to need separate A-and-D's for Phases Two and Three. But once he gets Phase

One off the ground, I don't think he'll need to play any more number games."

"And if he gets nailed, you could show me off to the prosecuting attorney. You didn't know what was going on, but you hired me to investigate when you got suspicious."

She mashed the cigarette out. "You make it sound worse than it is."

"You don't see it, do you?"

"See what?"

"You are risking everything on some slick hustler down from Canada, which is where he is going back to if this thing blows up. Preprinted or handwritten, your name is on those certificates, and they would crucify you. Birkett would be long gone, but you've got no place to hide. It's your fall. And maybe Walter Ravitt's. But he's smart enough to see it."

"That's how you found out about the certificates, through Walter?"

"He pointed me in the right direction."

She sat back. "How the hell did he know?"

"He's comptroller. He could get at least a peek at Birkett's A-and-D numbers. And Kristen probably dropped a few tidbits on their dates about how sales weren't going so good."

"Dates with Walter? That's not what I'd call it. Not that he didn't try."

And then, the question he did not want to ask. "Did Kristen know about the fake certificates?"

"It was her copy of the A-and-D application I found in her files when I took over."

"Was she in this with Birkett?"

"I don't know."

"I'm taking these certificates to an investigator in the state attorney's office."

"What? You can't *do* that! There's no real risk for investors. If Birkett gets in trouble, they'd just make him return the down payments."

"Investors would be lucky if they got twenty cents on the dollar. I don't want to see that couple I met in your office kiss every dime they have good-bye."

"If you go to the state with this, my career is over. You're as good as your reputation in this business, and if this gets out, I'm dead."

"Kristen *is* dead. And maybe this is the reason why."

She blinked. "Birkett? It doesn't make sense."

"How much is that A-and-D worth?"

"Fourteen million."

"I've seen people die for the loose change in their pockets. And if Birkett Gamble fed that shit to Kristen, I am going to burn him. Somehow, some way."

She put her head in her hands. "*Why* didn't I just let you stay in New York?"

He walked to the door. "Get on my side, Anne B. Johns."

He didn't need to go to Tallahassee to find an investigator for the state attorney. There was one in Kingston. His name was Jimmy Keye.

It being May and the dead season, Boomer hitched a ride. They took the coast road to Kingston, which gradually rose up out of the flat terrain. Downtown was mainly ten-story buildings bearing the names of banks surrounded by low-level shops, restaurants . . . and the ubiquitous Florida real estate office. The bank buildings all looked like they had opened yesterday.

"Mostly in the last five years or so," said Boomer. "Eighty percent of the drugs in this country come in through Florida. They can't build banks fast enough in this state. It's a real growth industry."

Jimmy Keye's office was in leased space in the headquarters of a bank. Axx and Boomer waited for an audience. After an hour they were ushered in. Jimmy Keye wore a white short-sleeved shirt and a thin brown tie. He looked harried.

"Which is Axx?" he said. Brad nodded. "You mentioned on the phone you are acting in some official role, Mr. Axx." An open folder on Keye's desk held his interest; he would look up at Axx, then back at the contents.

"Not exactly. I'm a detective, New York, but the problem is local."

"Local . . ."

"It involves some fake certificates issued as part of a real estate deal in Gulf Shores."

"Yes . . ." Keye moved a piece of paper from one side of the folder to the other. "Well, where is it being adjudicated?"

"It's not."

Keye now gave Axx his full attention. "It's *not?*"

"The certificates were just recently found to be fraudulent."

"By whom?"

"Me."

"When was that?"

"Yesterday." Axx explained the list, its origin, and its defects.

Keye regarded Boomer for the first time. His face wore an insincere smile. "And he wants me to launch an investigation, I bet you a dollar."

Said Axx, "This guy has already put in his pocket close to two million dollars actual buyers gave him. He is conning a bank to get fourteen million more. If the real estate project goes bad, everybody loses but him."

Keye looked down at the folder. He lifted it intact. "You see this, Mr. Axx? This is two guys in the contracting business who quote, renovated, unquote, the district courthouse. This work has been completed. They were paid. But the courthouse roof leaks. The stucco is cracking. When the toilets are flushed, it comes up instead of going down. The building department won't approve a certificate of occupancy." He lifted the folder. "This is sixty-seven million dollars of fraud."

"I'm sorry to hear that," said Axx. "Now, about River Woods—specifically what statute in Florida law has the developer violated, based on the evidence I presented here?"

Keye said nothing for a moment, then pushed a button on his telephone.

"Yes, Mr. Keye?"

"Mary, bring me your red file."

"The whole thing?"

"All of it."

"Right."

Shortly, an armful of folders were horsed into the office by a young woman, who let them thud onto Keye's desk. "Thank you, Mary. You can have them back in a few minutes."

When she had gone out, Keye said, "This is just one man. He opened an investment office five years ago. It was supposed to be part of a nationwide firm with a Dun and Bradstreet rating. It wasn't. He sold municipal bonds that supposedly had a triple-A rating. They didn't. What he sold was junk. To three thousand people who put up about twenty-five grand apiece, on average. In some cases this was their life savings. They pissed it down the tubes. Seventy-eight million dollars. They've been in court for four years in a class-action suit. They are trying to find him and their money."

Keye buzzed Mary, who laboriously retrieved her red file.

Jimmy Keye folded his hands in front of him. "Now, how many investors did you say were involved in this real estate deal, and how much money did they put up, and what action have they taken thus far to recover their funds, which, unless I am mistaken, they have not yet lost?"

It was now Axx's turn to talk to Boomer. "I don't think this man is interested in helping us. Does he sound to you like he's interested in helping us?"

"He sounds like he could give a—"

"Tell you what you do," said Jimmy Keye. "You send registered letters to every one of those names you say the developer put on bogus certificates. You tell them what you told me. You wait until you hear from them. You should allow three months for this. Then you call me with the results. Maybe we'll talk about an investigation. In the meantime I have better things to do."

Jimmy Keye turned a page in his folder.

"Guess we start mailing letters and sit around for three months," Axx said to Boomer.

"Looks like the only thing to do."

"Have you got a typewriter?"

"No."

"We'll need one."

"I can't type."

"Me neither."

The rustle of paper became more violent.

"I think he's getting pissed off," said Boomer.

"What pisses me off is the way he keeps looking at those papers the whole time we are in here."

Keye closed the folder and opened a drawer in the desk. He threw the folder in, slammed the drawer shut. "Okay, now catch the bus."

"That's better," said Axx, standing.

"Sure," said Boomer, also rising. "You don't mind doing something if people come right out and ask you in a nice way."

They waited in the air-conditioned hush of a marble hallway for an elevator.

"Down here, kid, there's no crime until they find blood."

Birkett Gamble stood at the stern, gazing across the wind-blown surface of the Gulf. Here it was, springtime, but at midday the sun seemed a tangible force. He adjusted a wide-brimmed panama hat and thought about the crisp coolness of Canada.

"Will you be fishing, sir?"

"No, Bobby, not today. Too damn hot."

The first mate drew a wristband across his forehead. "Fish thinking the same way. Sixty, here, and they're down fifty-nine-and-a-half. They might get hungry late afternoon."

The chairman of the town council was now coming up from below, where he had changed into one of the array of swimsuits Gamble kept available for guests on the *Lucky Strike,* a fifty-five-foot office, restaurant, lounge, and whatever served his purposes.

"I don't think our guest is interested in fishing, Bobby. Not in the water, that is."

"Hey there, Birkett! I am one thirsty sailor!"

Miles Kenyon, Sr., stepped onto the deck. He stood with great creamy expanse of belly happily overhanging his trunks. Gamble nodded to Bobby, who said, "What'll it be, sir?"

"It will be a Tom Collins, tall and lovely. And speaking of tall and lovely, what the hell happened to Carolyn?"

"She's getting comfortable, Miles. She'll be along."

"Ta-da!"

At the door leading below stood a blonde in a metallic gold bikini. She was posing for them like the model she occasionally was.

"Wow!" said Miles. "You get better looking every day, sweet thing."

Carolyn sauntered over to them and slipped an arm around the chairman's girth. She gave him a peck on the cheek, then slid away as he reached for her. She fanned herself with a hand. "Whew! Sure is hot."

Miles kept his eyes on her. "You need to get wet, darling."

"I believe that sounds like a fine idea."

Bobby brought the Tom Collins. Miles took a long deep draw. "Ahhhhh, ain't life grand?" He slapped his belly once, then caressed it in a slow circular motion.

Birkett raised his drink. "To the finer things in life, Miles." He cut his eyes at Carolyn, who began climbing a ladder to the deck above. Miles followed his gaze. The two men watched her run hands through golden hair, stretching until she was on tiptoes. Then she spread a towel and reclined on it, as previously instructed.

"Oh to be young again, Birkett."

Gamble waited a moment, then said, "I heard the news about Miles Junior. Congratulations."

"I didn't think that boy could find his butt with both hands. Now he's going to college."

"Josie's next, I guess."

"Two more years to go, but she's already looking. Then comes Billy. By that time, at least, I won't be carrying Miles Junior."

"It's a hardship. How's business?"

"A shade off from last year. Residential starts are down. Doesn't help me a bit. But that's business. No complaints. You just have to bear down and hustle harder."

"That's what I tell my brokers. People don't *buy*, they're *sold*."

Kenyon nodded vigorously. "These kids today don't want to hear it. They're waiting for somebody to walk up and ask, please, can I buy this?" They both laughed.

Offhandedly Miles Kenyon said, "What's First Gulf doing on your A-and-D?"

"They still look favorably upon our modest project. They await final approval by the council."

Miles tipped his glass up and emptied it. As he did so Birkett motioned toward the bar. In a few moments another drink arrived.

"Thank you," said the council chairman to the first mate. "I expect we'll have a quorum tonight, Birkett. Milner's back from Denver. Todd is home from Kern Memorial, all dried out for a few more months. I don't think that boy is going to be around for elections."

Garson Todd was Kenyon's swing vote on the council.

"Where do you stand with the subcontracts?" Kenyon asked.

"Five signed, three more in negotiation—one electrical, a very considerable one. All of them Gulf Shores vendors, naturally."

"A real shot in the arm for this town, what you're doing out there, Birkett."

A presentation by Gamble before the township planning board had already demonstrated in precise detail how big this boost would be. Gulf Shores electricians, roofers, concrete finishers, heavy-equipment operators, carpenters, masons, and the like were cheered by the prospect of 1,500 River Woods units under construction over three years.

"I believe in taking care of your own, Miles. Circulate the revenue. Keep it in the community."

Four miles of roads had already been cut into Phase One. Low bid of six thousand dollars per mile was by a contractor whose sister was the wife of Garson Todd, which was why Todd's illness so distressed Birkett Gamble. Sure, MFC had specified three-inch blacktop, which was like spraying black paint on sand; but with overruns, the job had cost thirty thousand. Birkett felt taken advantage of, which was often necessary but never satisfying. Then Garson Todd checks into the hospital to dry out just when the town council is getting ready to convene and officially bless River Woods. With Ed Milner out of town and Jim Kennedy away because of a death in the family, no quorum.

"Whiting was asking about the treatment plant," said Miles.

"What about it?" Gamble took note of the tone in which this was said and cautioned himself. But another voice told him he was tired of being yanked around, and it was time to tie down this end of River Woods.

"He's not sure about the cost analysis. He's strictly a numbers man, Birkett. I hate them myself, but it's hard to argue with them."

"Not if you have the correct numbers, and we do. We

laid this entire matter out for you people—for the planning commission, the zoning board, the department of public works, for anybody else who wanted to hear it."

"I know, Birkett, I know. Whiting saw your presentation. But he's worried the fees won't cover expenses. He's afraid the township will have to kick in somewhere down the road."

As part of the River Woods plan of development, Birkett Gamble proposed building a sewage treatment plant at MFC expense, then turning it over to the township. Also to be deeded to the township was a fifty-two-acre parcel on which the township would build a public safety center for police and fire services. There would be a school and a recreation area with tennis courts, exercise trails, and picnic grounds. Ongoing expenses for all of this would be covered by water and sewer fees paid by River Woods residents.

"Our analysis shows a surplus over anticipated expenses," said Gamble. "I really don't know where Whiting's getting his numbers."

"He's sincere, Birkett." By this Kenyon meant the man was not looking for anything.

Birkett contemplated the horizon. "I do think the proposal could be amended to include a reevaluation of the anticipated costs and a possible upward revision in user fees—two months prior to deeding the facility to the township."

This would cost Birkett Gamble nothing and the residents of River Woods more.

Kenyon sipped his Tom Collins. "It's a pleasure doing business with you, sir."

"Speaking of which . . ." Birkett went over to a small white table around which were set white canvas chairs.

On the table was an open briefcase. From it he lifted two sheaves of stapled legal-sized papers. He extended one without looking at the chairman, who seated himself and flipped through the pages disinterestedly.

"You sure got yourself a good price, Birkett."

"Purchase terms are as bid, Miles. Of course, there's no need for you to warehouse inventory. Just deliver and install."

When Kenyon heard this, he tossed the papers on the table. "Looks fine."

Birkett immediately signed his name to the last page of each copy of the contract by which Gulf Household, Inc., would furnish kitchen and utility-room appliances throughout River Woods, thus contributing greatly to the higher education of Josephine, William, and Miles Kenyon, Jr.

Like the road construction work at River Woods, the appliance contract had been bid out to forestall any charges of political favoritism.

Miles Kenyon, Sr., took pen in hand. He signed with a flourish. Birkett replaced the papers in the briefcase, which he snapped shut.

On the deck above, Carolyn yawned, then swung herself down the ladder.

"Well, look who's here!" said the council chairman.

Her brown body gleamed in the sun. Beads of perspiration had formed on a taut belly. She touched at them with her fingers. "It's so *hot.* . . ."

"Bobby!" Birkett called.

The first mate appeared.

"Another refreshment for our guest."

"I want to go for a swim," Carolyn complained.

"There are big fish out this far, honey bun," Kenyon said. "They could eat you up in one bite."

Bobby brought the drink, then went below. Birkett climbed the ladder to the wheelhouse.

Carolyn's lips formed a pout. "I need to get wet." Her eyes met the chairman's, held there. She glanced away, toward the wheelhouse, which was not visible, then back, smiling impishly. Her hands lazily reached back and the top of her bikini popped loose, hanging only by a string from her neck. She lifted this free and let it dangle from one hand as she spun about and strutted to a deck lounger, on which she now reclined.

Miles Kenyon watched her as he finished off his Tom Collins. He heard and felt the deep rumble of the twin diesels.

Carolyn lay in the sun up to her waist. Her bikini brief was secured by a pair of gold-tipped bows. Long fingers lightly held each tip. She looked at him. Her face was sullen; the coquette was vanished. He sat, as quiet as the sea around them. The bowstrings were straightened, then fell loosely. Her knees drew slowly up.

"Come over here, Miles."

Above, Birkett eased the big boat forward, swinging about to ninety-seven degrees SE. He brought her to five knots.

At this rate the *Lucky Strike* would not arrive dockside for an hour.


They were arrayed in a row at three long tables in the center of the stage in the high-school auditorium. There were five of them and the township clerk. Before each was set a microphone, next to which lay a white lined pad and a yellow pencil. The tables were discreetly draped in front. A tangle of wires leading to the microphones polluted the simple bureaucratic elegance of this ensemble.

The man seated in the middle spoke into his microphone. "I hereby open this special session of the governing council of the township of Gulf Shores for purposes of hearing final testimony and public comment on the plan of development for the residential subdivision known as River Woods."

He spoke too loudly. The amplified words of Miles Kenyon, Sr., rebounded through the big room, which was sparsely populated.

To the right of the stage was a clump of township officials with stapled pages of testimony in their laps. To the other side were a man in an open-necked shirt and a girl in jeans, each with notebook and pen at the ready: the local press. In the second row front, three young men in business suits were shoulder to shoulder behind Birkett Gamble, next to whom was yet another good-looking woman.

The chairman looked down and said, "Who's first up?"

Nobody moved. Then a tall bespectacled man in a light green suit made his way to a floor microphone positioned in the orchestra pit.

Wendell A. Weeks testified that the nine-hundred-acre site located in the north half section of range fifteen in the township, currently zoned for agriculture, had, after thorough review by the zoning board, been reclassified for residential usage, as requested by MFC, Inc.

Wendell was chairman of the zoning board.

Alan Samson compared the level of property taxes now yielded by River Ranch to the expected revenues to be collected from 1,500 residents of River Woods.

Alan was the township tax collector.

James R. Billings said the development plan for River Woods met every standard applicable, including a favorable environmental-impact evaluation by the state department of natural resources.

Jim was chairman of the planning commission.

Clement Highsmith communicated a glowing endorsement of the recreation facilities planned for the fifty-two-acre site to be deeded to the township by MFC upon completion of River Woods.

Clem headed up the department of parks and recreation.

A written statement by Winston P. Quist of the department of public works was read, regarding the considerable value of a sewage treatment plant constructed by MFC for the River Woods subdivision but owned and operated by the township and its skilled sanitation technicians.

Winnie was laid up with a bad back.

"Is he shoveling the stuff?" inquired Miles Kenyon of the woman to his left, who was the council clerk, Betty Quist. Her eyes did not reflect the amusement of her smile.

The chairman looked around. "This concludes testimony." Without enthusiasm he said, "The council will now hear public comment."

Reluctantly he surveyed the room. The covey of township officials, the MFC delegation, the reporters—he did not expect comment from any of these people. Inasmuch as the River Woods plan of development had been discussed ad nauseam in official forums for most of the past year, he did not expect public comment from any source this evening.

"The governing—"

Then he spotted the burly figure of Joe Bob Gates rise up midway back. Resignedly the chairman intoned, "Joe Bob . . ."

This man wore deep sideburns. A tattoo highlighted one biceps, clearly revealed when he folded his arms across his chest, rocking back on his heels. "It is my understanding that this big project, which will make a whole bunch of money for some people in this room, mostly everybody in this room, will have a lake." He waited.

Kenyon stared at him. "A lake?" Some of the people down front nodded. "Yes, that's right, a lake."

"How big?" said Joe Bob.

The chairman had no answer to this, nor did he wish to offer one. He wanted to hit Joe Bob with a stick. Instead he peered into the group of official bodies and said, "Well, Clem?"

The head of parks and recreation quickly got to his feet, papers sliding from his lap. He caught them and held them against a thigh as he said, "Thirty acres."

"Uh-huh," said Joe Bob. "And I understand this lake will be stocked with fishes."

"That is correct," said Clement Highsmith.

"How many?"

"This has not been discussed."

"Uh-huh. What kind?"

"We don't know yet. The kind with fins, I guess."

"No call for that, Clem," said Joe Bob. "Mr. Chairman—" He unfolded his arms and leaned on the back of the empty seat in front of him for added emphasis. "I propose the township council create a watchdog committee."

"To watch what?"

The reporters sniggered. Joe Bob was undeterred. "This committee should be charged with effectuating the proper amount and mix of freshwater species in this here lake, which I understand will be public in nature."

"A committee?"

"That's right. Local sportsmen should not come to this

place, when and if it ever opens, and everybody is trying
to catch maybe five catfish in the whole pond."

"A committee," said Kenyon.

"I volunteer to serve as chairman."

Kenyon quickly restated this proposition in an official
tone. "All in favor?"

A low murmur of yeas.

"All opposed, motion carried. It is so ordered. Clem,
you will be liaison."

Highsmith was not sure what this meant, but it sounded
like more work. He nodded sourly. Joe Bob Gates reseated
himself triumphantly.

The chairman now cleared his throat. "The governing
body of the township of Gulf Shores, Kern County,
hereby does approve the development of the River Woods
subdivision as set forth in the master plan submitted by
MFC Incorporated and reviewed and approved by the
appropriate township, county, and state authorities. The
buildings department is hereby ordered to issue a construction permit within one week to MFC Incorporated.
We further instruct township departments to expedite any
matters affecting satisfactory completion of this project by
the estimated date set forth in the River Woods plan of
development. All in favor?"

This brought five clear responses in the affirmative.

"All opposed, motion carried."

Miles Kenyon, Sr., then lifted a gavel and Birkett Gamble heard echo through the room the sound for which he
had been waiting fourteen long months. He let himself
bathe in the sweet satisfaction of suddenly traversing a
great distance, as if a chess piece had moved swiftly along
a board.

But only for a moment.

He turned to Anne Johns. He could barely contain his rage. "We're celebrating at the club, dear. I hope you'll join us."

"Well, I—"

"I'm so pleased."

The party was small—the three MFC attorneys, Walter Ravitt, Birkett, and Anne Johns. The attorneys were drinking margaritas and talking shop. Walter Ravitt was sipping white wine and saying nothing. Birkett said to Anne, "Come dear, let's get a breath of air."

They went onto a deck clinging to the exterior of the Peninsula Restaurant, which overlooked the Gulf. "Lovely evening," he said.

"Yes."

"This was a very important evening for MFC and River Woods. For all of us." He moved a step closer, felt the firm muscularity of her hip against his thigh.

"It all went perfectly," she said. Her gaze remained fixed to the west.

"Are you happy, my dear?"

"Of course."

"Then why are you talking to that nasty detective, Mr. Axx?"

So, Birkett knew. She didn't concern herself with how—it could have been Walter, or someone Axx talked to. It didn't matter. She had known he would find out. She expected it.

"I had to protect myself."

"From what, my dear?"

"From you, Birkett. Your A-and-D filing included a stack of owner certificates as proof of sales in Phase One. Eighty-six of them were false."

"That filing went directly to First Gulf. How did you—"

"In her previous life before River Woods, Kristen steered a lot of mortgage business to First Gulf. You make friends doing that. A friend called to congratulate her on the good sales numbers for Phase One. Kristen asked her for a copy of the A-and-D application. I found it in her files a few days ago. Birkett, some of those certificates have *my* name and license number printed on them. You had no right to put me at risk like that."

"There is no risk. You saw what happened tonight. The River Woods plan of development has been blessed by the town fathers. That should immensely please all our friends down at First Gulf. Once the loan is approved, the nonex- istent certificate owners call in their nonexistent guarantees and get back their nonexistent down payments. You then resell the certificates to walking, talking buyers."

"And what if there aren't enough of them?"

"There will be."

"We may be too far from Kingston for a lot of people, Birkett. They don't want to commute thirty or forty minutes on a desolate road like I-75. This isn't New York or Washington. They can still buy close to Kingston at a decent price."

"Not for what we're offering, not for an acre per homesite, and not five minutes from the Gulf. River Woods is going to be a marvelous success, my dear. We may have to work harder to sell it, but we *will* sell it. I have no doubts. If I did, I would not have invested every last cent I have in it. You know as well as I do, Kingston is one of the fastest growing SMAs in the state. River Woods is going to grow with it."

"I think it will, but it's not going to happen overnight. I'm willing to ride the tough times out. I tied my career to

River Woods. But then you go and crap on the Florida real estate code, not to mention federal and state banking laws. I have to start looking out for myself, Birkett."

"You know, my dear, those are almost the exact words of your predecessor."

She looked away, at the thin line of surf curling onto white beach, which seemed luminescent in moonlight. He moved directly behind her. "It seems I underestimated both of you. But there are always choices. You have made yours." His fingers traced along her bare shoulder. "The question is, what are mine? I now have a detective from New York on my hands, whom I'd assumed we were fortuitously rid of."

"That's your problem, Birkett."

His face showed disappointment. "I thought you were right for River Woods, my dear. I thought you were a risk taker. You must live on the edge to make it big in this business. There is no payoff for finishing back in the pack."

"I don't intend to."

She felt his lips brush against her skin. "I recommend you begin looking for employment elsewhere. Perhaps at one of the agencies in town, where you will be assigned a desk in a roomful of many desks and spend most of your days looking for listings. Which I greatly regret."

She gathered her strength and turned to face him. "You can't dump me like that, Birkett."

Anger flashed in his eyes. His voice had an edge to it she hadn't heard before. "I picked you out of nowhere, I gave you a franchise to print money. And you treat what I did for you like garbage. You turn some cop loose on me and my company, *my* company!"

She now had no doubt he had hired two thugs to attack

Brad. She told herself that she must in no way show what she was feeling. It was too late to turn back now. She looked not at his eyes but at a point directly between. "That detective thinks you killed Kristen."

"Oh, does he?"

"He's a lot like you, Birkett. He likes to get what he goes after."

"Be extremely careful that you are not caught in the middle, my dear. It could be quite . . . painful."

"I think I'm safely on the sidelines now."

Birkett smiled thinly. "In these matters, innocent bystanders are often injured . . . as well as not-so-innocent ones."

A moment later she was alone in the darkness. She shuddered as the sea breeze gusted.

$\triangledown$

# CHAPTER SEVEN

BRAD Axx stood before the secretary of the president of First Gulf Bank. She was on the phone. He waited. She hung up. "May I help you?"

"I am sure of it. I need to speak with Mr. Watt immediately. It's urgent."

"What is this in reference to, Mr. . . . .?"

"Axx. It's urgent, but it's also confidential. Police business."

"Oh, well, uh—" She turned about and peered through the bronze-tinted glass that enclosed two sides of the president's office. He was seated at his desk looking at some papers. She lifted the telephone handset again, pressed a button on the console. "There is a Mr. Axx to see you, about a . . . police matter." She nodded and delicately replaced the receiver on the console. "You may go in."

"When I'm sure, I'm always right."

He went around her desk and along a corridor. It was formed on one side by the see-through wall of the president's quarters and on the other by a series of low partitions. These separated office cubicles inhabited by less exalted personnel. From one came sharp clacking sounds.

Through an open door he saw a young woman with very red hair tapping rapidly at the keyboard of a computer. She looked up and smiled as he went past. He turned into the office of Arthur Watt, who did not stand. Watt motioned him to a chair and said, "What can I do for you, Mr. Axx? You're police, are you?"

"New York type."

The president put the papers aside. "A long way from home."

"I've begun to think of Gulf Shores as a second home. So many wonderful things have happened to me since I came here."

"When was that?"

"A week or so ago."

An eyebrow lifted. "You must be getting around town."

"I'm already invested."

"Congratulations. Where?"

"River Woods."

"Getting in the door early, are you?"

"Your bank has an interest in River Woods."

"We're considering it, yes."

"I have something else for you to consider." Axx handed him the list of certificate owners. "They match up with copies Birkett Gamble filed with you for an A-and-D loan. Those check marks mean the certificates are bogus. The people don't exist, or they know squat about River Woods. Most of them are from outside Gulf Shores."

"How do you know this?"

"I went visiting, mainly in Ennisville. Ennisville is not what you would call an upscale community of flush investors looking for a sure thing."

"No, I wouldn't say it was. But Birkett *is* marketing River Woods as a community for working-class people."

"Many of the people on that list are no longer working because they are dead. Or they never worked because they never lived. Or they are working at jobs that couldn't carry the payments for a two-car garage in River Woods. They park on the front lawn."

"I see. And you yourself are an investor in River Woods?"

"Disgruntled."

"I see."

Axx explained the code Gamble had devised to separate the fake certificate holders from the real ones. "This way he could tell which certificates had to be resold. If you just looked at the certificates, you wouldn't see any pattern. This bank didn't."

To which the banker replied, "Well, I must say this news is very disturbing."

"I would be seriously pissed off if I were you."

"Our view of Mr. Gamble and his plan of development has been entirely favorable. We received copies of certificates representing, we thought, actual sales. How did you obtain this list?"

"Trade secret."

"Yes. Well, this certainly will require some looking into. I want to thank you for bringing this matter to our attention, Mr. Axx. Have you showed this list to the local authorities?"

Axx was not pleased by this question. "An investigator for the state attorney has seen it."

"And what did he say?"

"He said, go away."

"He didn't think anything of it?"

"No, he just wants to wait until there is blood on the floor before he goes to work. Are you Type A or O, Mr. Watt?"

On the way out he stopped in the door of the noisy cubicle. "You can really play that piano."

She leaned back and sighed. "I wish it did make music. We might get along better."

"You probably wouldn't like the sounds it made."

"Actually it *does* make sounds. A little beep every time you do something wrong. And then it talks to you, on the screen. It says, *'What?'* Insulting little creep."

"What do you do with it?"

She looked closely at him, then figured it was okay. This was a prized ability of Brad Axx: people of all shapes and sizes somehow figured it was safe to talk to him. Sometimes it was.

"My title is account manager reporting to the director of data processing. Which makes me a glorified clerk riding a computer instead of a paper trail."

"What accounts do you manage?"

"Corporate."

Arthur Watt came out of his office and shot them a long look as he passed by. She stuck her tongue out after him. "He doesn't think anybody around here does any work but him. He watches me all day long. He can't see me when I'm at my machine, which is a really lousy reason to work hard." Her lips were very full.

"He's a dirty old man."

"Are most men that way when they get older?"

"I'm that way already."

She blushed and wheeled her chair closer to the keyboard.

"By the way, I'm Brad Axx."

"Ginny Nye."

"See you again."

"Bye."

The Gulf Shores Yacht Club began at the end of a red brick road leading to a gate. Next to the gate was a circular building topped by a copper spire. Outside the building stood a small thin boy in an outsized uniform that made him look like a very tan but undernourished doorman on Park Avenue. He held a clipboard in a white-gloved hand.

"Yes, sir?" He looked in at Axx and his passenger. He looked twice at the passenger.

Axx showed him his shield.

"Yes, sir."

A button was pressed and the yellow gate swung up and held.

"Thanks. Where is Mr. Gamble's boat parked?"

"Fifty-two. To your right."

In his side mirror, as he accelerated, Axx watched the boy look after him, then write on a pad attached to the clipboard. He swung right and saw the expression on the face of his passenger.

"What's the matter with you, eat some bad grouper?"

"You don't park a boat, Brooklyn. You moor it, or you dock it, or you tie it up, but you don't park the mother."

"You think I never saw a boat before? And that kid was eyeballing you, Boomer, not me."

"The kid was on the job."

"By the way, where do you dock your yacht?"

"I had to sell it."

Axx eased along a row of very large boats separated only by narrow catwalks. "The rich can put distance between their houses, but not their boats."

"Until they get out to sea," said Boomer. "And in aircraft carriers like these, they can get as far as they want to go."

On a craft of this description they saw a group of people gathered. Among them, in white pants, red-striped shirt, and white captain's hat, was Birkett Gamble.

"There's our boy," said Axx.

"Very nautical."

A wiry man who looked like he belonged on a boat met them just as they were about to board. "That's all right, Bobby, they're welcome." Birkett Gamble had a drink in one hand and in the other a blonde in a black bikini. "Would you gentlemen care for anything from the bar?"

"No thanks," said Axx.

"A beer," said Boomer.

Axx shot him a glance, which went unnoticed. Boomer was concentrating on the blonde.

"What brings you down to the sea, Mr. Axx?"

"I need to check my heading, Mr. Gamble. I think I'm right on course, but I want to make sure."

"On course for what?"

"Nailing you to the wall."

The blond's face dropped. Birkett didn't miss a beat. "I think this conversation should be private in nature, don't you?" He turned to the girl. "Please excuse us, my dear. I trust you'll be able to amuse Mr. Axx's companion."

As Axx and Gamble went below, Axx heard Boomer say, "I'm looking for a girl with a beautiful body and a sick mind."

The cabin looked like somebody's living room. Gamble sank into a sofa. Axx examined the home entertainment system.

"Perhaps you would enjoy a tour of my modest craft?"

Axx was led through the galley, which was about the size of an eat-in kitchen in most New York apartments. They went forward, where Birkett opened a hatch leading

up to the bow. What he referred to as the head was directly
below. "I always say, let the sun shine in." This was meant
as a joke. Axx did not laugh. Gamble pulled the hatch
down and locked it. As he turned away Axx reached up
and slid the handle in the opposite direction. They returned to the main cabin.

Gamble seated himself, crossed his legs, and said, "Now
what the hell do you mean coming on my boat and
insulting me in front of my guests?"

"Is that what she is?"

"Carolyn is an acquaintance."

"Was Kirsten an acquaintance?"

Pale blue eyes searched Axx's face. "She was a close
friend and colleague."

"She is a dead close friend and colleague."

"Which I understand is the likely outcome when one
indulges in that form of vice."

"So you agree with the chief of police—accidental
death?"

"Chief Snow is a reasonable man."

"But I am not. I get ideas like this—Kirsten learned
about the phony certificates you peddled over at First
Gulf, trying to get your A-and-D money. You panicked
and took her out."

"Absurd."

"When I started sniffing around, you send a couple of
pit bulls after me."

"I heard someone tried to rough you up, Axx. I can't
imagine why. But it's not my style. You see, I can get
what I want without it."

Axx ignored this disclaimer. "But somewhere along the
line Kirsten found something more damaging to you, and
more dangerous to her."

"Precisely what, might I ask?"

"Who Walter Ravitt is fronting for. The shareholder who doesn't want his name in the public record."

"A silent partner? Oh, how quaint!" He laughed delightedly. "There is no silent partner, detective. I reincorporated down here from Canada shortly before I found River Ranch. Later I decided it would be best to list more than one officer—in addition to my wife, I mean. A bank takes you more seriously. And I was going to ask a bank for a lot of money. I had no partner, so I used Walter and compensated him for it. That's all there is to that, I'm afraid."

"And I am telling you Kristen found more than the sham paper you shopped at First Gulf."

"I suppose by this hypothesis I had to silence her. I did this by forcing her to consume a great quantity of cocaine."

Axx looked past him at a pennant snapping soundlessly in the wind. "Nobody had to force cocaine on Kristen." His gaze returned to Birkett Gamble. "And it didn't take much to kill her, not the brand you supplied."

"That accusation is outrageous. I do not use drugs, I know nothing about drugs, and I certainly did not supply drugs to Kristen. I knew she used them. I saw her use them. She liked to do cocaine in bed with me. In fact, she had to have it then."

"Maybe she needed it then."

The smirk dissolved. "Kristen killed herself because she was weak. She simply could not cope. A character flaw. As far as River Woods goes, it's right on schedule. If you were smart, you'd take every dollar you stashed away off the pad up in New York and buy in big."

Axx grabbed Birkett Gamble by his seaman's shirt, causing the captain's hat to tumble off.

"Mister, I am on your case for the duration. I am going to crawl up your ass and give you indigestion." He released his grip and Gamble flopped back into the confines of the couch. "For starters, I delivered that list of certificate holders to Arthur Watt today."

Birkett Gamble readjusted his garments. "You've absolutely spoiled my day, Axx. It's going to be another sleepless night. Now, if you have nothing else to say to me, would you please get the hell off my boat?"

Axx found Boomer off in a corner with the blonde in the black bikini. A lacquered fingernail toyed with bushy sideburns.

"Excuse me, Pop, but we have to get going. You're late for your blood test."

"Blood test?" said the blonde.

"It's been nice talking with you," said Boomer. "Now I have to return this social leper to his colony."

"The boss said he wants some alone time," Axx told her. "He said to get everybody off the boat.'

*"What?"*

In the car Axx pounded the wheel as he sped off. "I am going to get that bastard a court date he will not walk away from."

Boomer said, "This is the way you do things up in New Yawk? Go straight at them until they fall down dead?"

"It's the only way I know how. Sooner or later they fall."

"Are you sure you know who *they* are?"

Axx kept his eyes on the road.

"Corruption in Florida is intricate and unique," said Boomer. "Just when you think you're there, you're not."

The security gate jerked open. Axx nodded to the uniformed boy as he cruised out.

Boomer said, "I liked that one about checking your heading. Where'd you pick that up?"

"Bluefishing with the old man on *Big Mama Two,* out of Sheepshead Bay. Five bucks, all day."

Walter Ravitt sat at a table by the window in the Peninsula. He had been waiting twenty minutes, and was growing annoyed, when the seat opposite became occupied.

"Hello, Walter. I hope you've been having a good day, because I've got some bad news."

"I've been having a lousy day."

"Eighty-six of the River Woods certificate holders don't exist. I turned the list over to First Gulf."

Ashen, the comptroller considered the consequences of this. "I guess that puts River Woods under three feet of water and me with it."

"You can get another job. You won't take the rap."

"That's makes me feel better, Axx."

"Unless . . ."

"Unless what?"

"What made you think Birkett was running a shell game on First Gulf?"

The answer came without hesitation. "Kristen is telling me sales have slowed, and they weren't all that great from the start—respectable, but not great. The A-and-D filing is around the corner. I'm thinking we might not get the money. But Birkett is saying, 'Don't worry, we'll have the numbers.' And he did. I had serious reservations about their authenticity."

"What did he say when you asked him about it?"

Ravitt snorted. "Are you kidding? I might as well ask for a kick in the head. I don't have to tell you, he can be a dangerous man."

"He says he's against violence in principle. He says he doesn't need it."

"You believe him?"

"He's never lied to me before. So you decided to do what, Walter, stick your head in the beach?"

"I decided to keep my mouth shut and do my job. I was going to wait it out and pray. Then you show up asking questions about incorporation papers and MFC."

"And the first thing you do is run to Birkett."

"I told you, I was worried. You come on strong, Axx, to put it mildly. Birkett dislikes details but he always knows the lay of the land. I figured I better fill him in before he hears I'm talking to you and I'm out on the street. He didn't seem upset."

"He was."

"I had no idea he would send those guys after you, honest to God."

"I knew you were sorry about it. You became my little helper."

"In my position, wouldn't you? I could go down with Birkett's ship. I decided I had to find out what Birkett was doing at MFC. I'm listed as an officer, you know that. Which means I'm liable."

"For more than you think."

"What does *that* mean? What *else* is that lunatic up to?"

"You tell me, Walter."

"Dammit, Axx, I gave you everything I had, which wasn't much, I admit. But you found proof Birkett was falsifying sales figures, which is just what I was afraid of. You're saying there's more to it than that?"

"I am saying it's about Kristen."

"Oh geezus." Ravitt motioned to the waitress.

"When did you last see her?"

"We came here to iron out a few wrinkles over drinks. When I left, she was still here, with Birkett."

"Where did you go?"

"Home."

"How do I know that?"

"Check my doorman." He reddened. "And my, uh, secretary was with me that night."

"Walter, you devil you."

"I couldn't get anywhere with Kristen."

"Birkett beat you to it?"

"I'm no competition for Birkett Gamble."

"How long had she been using?"

"Using what?"

"What killed her, Walter."

"I never saw her with it. She'd get depressed and then kind of hyper, but I figured that was the pressure of the job. Real estate is crazy, it can turn your life into a yo-yo." His drink arrived and he took a quick swallow. "Gamble killed Kristen? But the police said it was a drug overdose."

"She had to be getting her stuff from someone. He fed her a grade that would take out a horse."

"Why?"

"If you have information about Birkett's business dealings I should know about, Walter, you better unload. You may not get another chance. From me or Birkett."

Ravitt lifted a napkin and dabbed at the sheen on his forehead. "That is a hell of a thing to tell me, Axx."

"I'm just a hell of a guy, Walter."

"I *can't* help you! MFC is a one-man show and Birkett is the man. I thought he was a genius. I still think so, but I wish I'd never met him."

"MFC . . . what do the letters stand for?"

"Nothing, as far as I know. Mighty Fine Corporation, maybe."

"Or something closer to the truth. You think about what I told you. You get any ideas, call me at Boomer's."

"The idea I'm thinking about is getting out of this podunk town as fast as I can."

"That would not look good, Walter. That would not look good at all."

Axx left him musing glumly and went to the bar. The bartender dropped a cardboard coaster in front of Axx.

"I'm not drinking. I'm asking."

"Asking what?"

"Who works Monday nights?"

"Mondays? Me."

"You're the day man."

"I take a double. Barnes can't make it Mondays, the wimp."

"Did you know Kristen McCauley?"

"I knew Kristen."

"She was here one Monday night not long ago. With some people from River Woods."

"That's right. They been in before."

"Who waited on their table?"

"I did."

"You?"

"They were over there, in the corner. That table and the one next to it are mine, 'cause they're close to the bar."

"This is what I am really asking. Did she leave alone, or did she go out with someone?"

"She left with Mr. Gamble."

"About what time?"

"Eleven or so."

"You have a good memory."

"I had to break a hundred for him to pay for their drinks. He left twenty on the table. Yeah, I remember them."

Axx withdrew a twenty-dollar bill from his wallet. "For the memory."

It was the third door he knocked on. The first was opened by a man who said he had been away on business for three weeks and returned yesterday. At the second nobody answered. Now he was rapping on this one. Three strikes and you're—

"Yes?" The door remained shut.

"I'm a friend of Kristen McCauley. Can I speak with you a moment?"

Various locks were released. It was a touch of old New York. The door opened in stages and he looked down at a hunched woman in a flowery housecoat. Hair like steel wool was pulled tight behind her head. His expectations trended downward. This woman was not likely to be awake during the hours Kristen kept, but he hoped she might be that most valuable of commodities—a watcher.

"I'm investigating Miss McCauley's death."

"A murder?" She seemed delighted.

"Possibly."

"And *I'm* a suspect?"

"Not at all."

"Oh." She perhaps expected to go downtown for questioning. That would break up the day.

"I'm trying to determine when Kris—Miss McCauley arrived home the night she died and if she was alone. Do you remember that evening?"

"I remember all the police cars and ambulances the next

morning. They carried that poor girl out in a big black bag. It was terrible." Her eyes cut across the street. "We were all over there. She was young, so very *young.*" In her tone was regret and triumph.

"Did you notice the time she came home? It was a Monday night."

"Monday is canasta night at the clubhouse. Wilma and Bernice got angry because I won. I keep track of what's played and they don't. So I beat their butts. Is that my fault?" She lifted her chin defiantly.

"You should have retired to Atlantic City."

She beamed. "You were asking me about . . . oh yes, that night. And that girl. She came in late, very late."

"You saw her?"

"I can never sleep after we play, and Wilma and Bernice got me upset. So I sat on the porch and read. I saw her."

"Was she alone?"

"Yes."

Axx looked out the window at Kristen's villa. "Wasn't it dark?"

"She always leaves the front light on when she goes out. I could see. My chair is by the porch window."

"You said it was very late. Any idea what time?"

"Let's see. We played until nine-thirty. Then I came home and watched the end of that Gable movie, about eleven. Then I went to bed. I remember I got up around twelve and warmed some milk. That didn't work, so I got up again, it must have been about one o'clock."

"When you began reading?"

"No, when she came home. I was reading maybe fifteen minutes and heard her car."

"What color was it?"

"Blue. Light blue. My, she was so pretty and—"

"Did you see her?"

"*See* her?"

"Get out of the car?"

"It was her car. I figure it was her."

"There was just the driver?"

"Yes"

"But she didn't get out of the car?"

"She had one of those thingamajigs. The garage door went up, then it went back down. You're not supposed to have to get out of the car. That's the point of—"

Axx thanked her for her time and assistance.

So Kristen left the Peninsula around ten o'clock with Birkett Gamble and did not arrive home until three hours later. Alone.

A truck turned the corner and stopped in front of the McCauley villa. On its side in large letters read: MAIN MART. WE BUY ANYTHING. ESTATES OUR SPECIALTY. Axx watched the driver and his helper climb down and trudge to the front door. The driver had a key. They left the door open.

At a certain point in homicide cases Brad Axx played a mind game with himself: the victim was still living by the fact of Axx's investigation. Axx would learn every detail of this life—habits, preferences, friends, enemies. In his search no one was yet dead. The search must succeed. As if by this, what had happened would not happen—he would know the killer; there would be no victim.

He looked at the door casually left open by the men who had come to remove Kristen's belongings.

This case was different. The mind game did not work with this one. It did not have to. He had found something else.

▽

# CHAPTER EIGHT

She was about to push off when he arrived. She wore a pair of white shorts, a white shirt, and black high-top sneakers. Her body was short and muscular. It did not look sixty years old or thereabouts. He couldn't see much of her face: her hat was equipped with flaps, which were in the down position; her sunglasses were a wraparound windshield. She was going fishing.

"Janice Kern Gamble?"

"You found her."

She stood in a boat considerably less grandiose than the one the Gambles kept at the Gulf Shores Yacht Club. It was low and wide and not very long. There were two seats raised up like stools at a lunch counter. On the stern was a large motor, maroon with rust. Axx watched her try to start this in the same fashion the guys in Bensonhurst fired up their lawnmowers. She got about the same results.

"Sheeoot!"

"My name is Brad Axx. I'd like to talk to you before you leave."

"Bass feed with the cows, Mister. I don't mind wasting time, but I like it to be on the water. What do you want to talk about?"

"Your husband."

"I'm here to have a good time."

Axx laid down his bet. "I'm here to put him in jail."

This caught her in midyank. She peeled away the wrap-around windshield and looked him over. "Why don't you come aboard and put some of that muscle to work?"

He climbed down into the boat, which listed danger-ously. "Always step into the middle," she advised. He grabbed hold of the crank handle and gave it his best shot. The engine roared. She let go the lines and they headed upriver, racing across the onyx surface at what felt like a hundred miles an hour. In shallow water she cut the power. They drifted near the bank. He was handed a rod with the reel set underneath.

"You fish?" she asked.

"Out of Sheepshead Bay."

"Where?"

"Brooklyn."

She looked at him crookedly, then demonstrated the proper technique for spinning tackle. At the end of his line was an odd-looking strip of something.

"Pork rind."

They cast into the grasses by the riverbank.

"I've been fishing this spot since I was a little girl. My daddy brought me here. That house you passed by?" He had noticed it: small and red and set about a foot off the ground, resting on what looked to be concrete blocks. "He built that himself. Didn't have to, could have paid some contractor to come in and put up a mansion. But he didn't want to change this place. Out here everybody builds their own, and so did Daddy. He was a millionaire but he wore mail-order specs and his hands were as rough as a gator's back hide."

Axx noticed something moving in the grasses and
thought it might be a fish. He reeled in and got ready to
cast. It was no fish. It slithered along the surface, head
erect, rattles too, lifted high and dry. It skimmed regally
past without a glance at the intruders.

"Diamondback," she said. "Cottonmouths out here,
too. Watch where you reach."

"How did he make his money, your father?"

"He didn't make it, he kept it. Granddaddy made it. He
had a string of commercial boats fishing the Gulf. In those
days you could fish with an oar. Just hit the water with it.
The railroad wheeled their boxcars right up to the fish
houses, then headed north. Granddaddy liked money and
loved politics. They named the county after him in oh-
nine. Hurricane of twenty-one wiped out everything:
boats, nets, fish houses."

There was an explosion of water in the grasses. Her rod
bent and she snapped it back. The lure popped free. "The
little slickster." She cast again.

"Did he rebuild?"

"No money for that. And the banks didn't like the risk.
Not that he was broke. He'd put his cash into land. So he
quit being a fisherman and started being a citrus farmer.
Taught the business to Randolph, my daddy. Daddy's
only problem was, he had a daughter and not a son. One
day he just dropped. I ran things for a while, but I needed
help. I married, but that was no help a'tall."

A fish jumped, silvery in the fading sun. She was
unimprssed. "What we want is a lot bigger."

Beyond the riverbank was a tufted palm soaring on a
thick trunk. "Cabbage palm," she said. "Good eating."

"You *eat* a palm tree?"

"A few years before this place got crowded, a Yankee swell on vacation looked down his nose at a cracker boy in coveralls and bare feet and said, 'What do you live off down here?' The boy said, 'Gators and cabbage palms in the summer, sick Yankees in the winter.' "

"This Yankee wants to know, how do you eat a palm tree?"

"You climb up top young trees and cut out the cabbage hearts. You could eat them raw, but Mama steamed them with salt pork and onions. She'd fix some fried bream and willow cats with it. Daddy knew what he was doing when he married. More than I can say for myself."

They fished and drifted. He knew Florida as white sand, and yellow sun, green trees. Now he saw color he had not noticed—a splash of crimson in the branches of a live oak.

"Air plants."

"Who plants?"

"No roots. Storm blows in, you're walking on them next day."

It was no fault of his the bass managed to hook itself. It jumped, twisting against the line, once, then again. It fought all the way to the boat, where she scooped it up in a net. She worked the lure loose from a mouth that looked wider than the fish.

"Now you know why they call them largemouth."

She dumped it in the fish box, cast out. "Can't let some New York boy outfish me."

"Does Birkett fish?"

"He's got some fancy fishing poles on that big boat of his. For his so-called friends."

"You don't go on it?"

"This is my country, back in here. He does business on the boat. I don't much like who he does it with, or the way he does it."

"He seems pretty good at it. A bona fide wheeler-dealer."

"That's why he came down from Canada. The government was killing him up there. You should hear him talk about it. Taxes, regulations. If you've got an hour, ask him about when they passed a law that everything had to be in two languages, English and French."

"So he came to Florida."

"About as far from Canada as you can get in these United States, any way you look at it." She sighed. "And I fell for him."

"He does have style."

"There's less there than meets the eye, mister. Why are you after him?"

"I think he caused the death of one of the people who worked with him."

"That girl?"

"Yes."

"But you can't prove it or you wouldn't be in this boat with an old woman trying to catch bass."

"I can't prove it yet. Murder needs motive. This motive has something to do with River Woods."

"I don't know much about River Woods. That's all Birkett."

"You're not invested?"

"For years I thought men wanted to marry me for my money. So I get hooked up with one I think has his own. Wrong, Janice."

"But Kristen told me he's got a half million tied up in River Woods."

"Birkett made money in garden apartments outside Toronto. Then he went into shopping centers, a couple small ones, then a big one. The big one isn't doing so

well. There are people in Toronto who are looking for
Birkett Gamble. They are getting ready to go into court
down here. I didn't know any of this until my lawyer filled
me in last week. I talked to my lawyer too late, as he keeps
reminding me."

"Lawyer?"

"Divorce, mister."

A thud and rumble sounded to the east. Axx saw thick
black clouds where seemingly moments earlier there had
been blue sky. "That doesn't look good," she said. "Better
reel in."

They were back at the dock in fifteen minutes. She
handed him the rods, tossed the fish up onto the grass. As
he ran a hose over the boat she said, "It's my lawyer's
opinion that Birkett married me for two reasons—my
money and my name. He got some money from me for
River Woods. But my name . . . Daddy used to say the
Kern name was good as gold. Birkett's been trading on
that name and I'm going to cut him loose from it."

"How much did you give him for River Woods?"

"You don't mind asking anybody anything, do you?"

"I am playing for keeps, like your husband. I noticed
you were an officer in his company."

"I gave Birkett two hundred thousand dollars, fool that
I am."

"What did he do with it?"

"Half went down on the option he took a year ago, the
other hundred for a model home and sales office, architect
fees, road construction. . . . These projects are expensive
even in the planning stages, I found out."

"How much of his own money did Birkett put into
River Woods?"

"He made the second option payment—two-seventy."

"Why did he wait so long to get his own money working?"

"He wasn't liquid, he said. He had to sell off some holdings in Toronto, he said."

"Walter Ravitt is one of your fellow officers. Do you know him?"

"I should hope so. He worked for Stump and Stiles. They handle my finances. Walter took care of my taxes. He's from Ohio, but he went to college down here. When I got married, he started doing some work for my husband. Next thing I know, he's on the board."

"When did that happen?"

"Oh Lord, I don't remember. Let's see . . . around October, I think it was."

"Just before Birkett made the second option payment?"

"Yes, as a matter of fact."

"Didn't you vote on electing Walter Ravitt to the board of directors?"

"By then I didn't give a damn what the so-called board did. I knew about Carolyn and what Birkett was doing on that yacht, which is leased by the corporation, by the way. Did you think it was his?"

"I didn't ask."

"Well, if you want to go for a ride on it, you better do it soon. He hasn't been making his payments. That says everything about Birkett Gamble."

"If you weren't going to board meetings, how could Birkett run the company?"

"I told him he could do what he wanted with the company, but not to expect any more money out of me. I kept my shares but I gave him my proxy."

"I understand you knew Kristen McCauley."

"A lovely girl. And very . . . ambitious."

"She died of a cocaine overdose."

"I heard as much."

"Is your husband involved with drugs, Mrs. Gamble?"

"Birkett is 'fraid to take an *aspirin*."

"Last Monday, the night she died, do you remember it?"

"Monday nights is the Lee River Conservation Society, at the library."

"And after that?"

"Home."

"Here?"

"In town. That apartment of ours is mine, too."

"When did your husband come in?"

"I didn't hear him. Never do. He's in another bedroom. All I know is, he was home in the morning when the police called. Any more questions?"

"No, ma'am." He had already confirmed Ravitt's alibi: Walter was home by eleven.

"Look here, you go ahead after Mr. Gamble. I intend to be Janice Kern again as soon as I can. For all I care, Birkett Gamble can get the whole nine yards. He deserves it." She scooped up the bass. "You want this?"

"What I could use is a good steak."

She shook her head sadly. "Yankees . . ."


The boy peered at Axx from under the brim of his cap. Axx said, "Remember this face?"

"Yes, sir." He reached for the button by which the gate would be released.

"I'm not going in. It's you I want to talk to."

"Me?"

"You have something I need."

"I do?"

"You put it on that clipboard you carry."

The boy regarded the object under discussion as if for the first time.

"You keep a record of every car that goes in and out. I'd like to see the sheet for last Tuesday."

"I think you should talk with the security manager."

Axx extended a bill. "We can take care of this right now."

The bill disappeared into a pocket of the uniform. Inside the security station the boy opened a desk drawer. He began thumbing through papers. "Here." He handed Axx a report. "We write down the tags."

"The what?"

"The tags on the car."

"You mean the license-plate numbers?"

"Yeah, the tags."

"Okay, what's the tag for Birkett Gamble?"

"RWOODS."

Axx scanned the column headed "Incoming." Toward the bottom he found it: RWOODS. Time: 2327. So Birkett arrived at 11:27 P.M. Another car was right behind him, at 2328.

"This one, do you know whose plate this is?"

"Huh?"

"Who does this tag belong to?"

"That's the blonde in the blue Buick. She comes here now and then. She is one fine fox."

Axx now checked the parallel column, "Outgoing." Kristen's departure was listed as 2351, Birkett's as 0022. She was on the boat about twenty minutes—long enough to have a little chat before she packed up her snow and split. Gamble stuck around for another half hour. Axx wanted to go aboard that boat and tear it apart. Janice

Kern Gamble had said her husband was afraid to take an aspirin. Smart dealers don't use, and a yacht that size is a fine place to stash. If the climate warms up, you jettison.

But if Kristen was carrying, why didn't she head home? Her villa was ten minutes away, but according to her neighbor she didn't roll in until one o'clock in the morning.

Axx returned the sheet to the boy. "Thanks."

"You want me to let you know if I see that blonde again?"

"She left town."

"Too bad."

"Yeah."

The sun lay along the tree line as Axx rocketed down U.S. 31. An hour—where had Kristen spent it? She likely had done a line or two of weaker stuff on Birkett's boat. She was flying high, riding this same road around midnight.

He would go look for her.

First stop: Pier 7, restaurant/lounge/disco on the river. The bartender was the hottest number in the joint, nor did she make an effort to conceal her most remarkable assets.

"Hi, what'll it be?" Jennifer gave all new arrivals a big smile; the male ones usually didn't notice, their attention focused elsewhere.

Axx went right to work.

"What's the matter," Jennifer responded, "this Kristen chick do you a bad one?"

"She took a wrong turn."

She leaned forward. "Sweetheart, my advice to you is, don't get mad, get even."

A lieutenant in vice had once told Axx, if you want more trouble than you can handle, get hooked up with the

best-looking woman you can find. This bartender probably could prove him right. Kristen had.

He got in his car and drove downtown to the Libation
Station. He inquired of this bartender, who wore an ear-
ring but otherwise bore no resemblance to Jennifer, ex-
cepting an impressive chest. This one had hair on it.

"I don't talk to no pigs."

Axx felt better. This suited his mood. "You have a
problem," he said. "Your mouth overloads your ass."

He was formulating a plan of action to the response he
expected when he heard someone say, "Shut up, Brian."
And then to Axx, softly, "Sir, I am afraid I did not see
Miss McCauley in here for some months." This was
spoken by a pudgy man about twenty years older than the
bartender who wore multicolored shorts and matching
shirt topped off by an untropical beret.

"You're here until closing?"

"Every night. I own the place." The bartender hovered
three feet away. "Brian, don't you have some glasses to
wash?"

"They're all washed."

"Good. Go polish them."

Brian scowled and moved reluctantly away.

"Before he goes off to brood, I should determine if you
require a libation, sir."

"I'm fine."

The owner contemplated his own libation, which was
tall and colorful and had a small umbrella sticking out of
it. "I always try to pick who I'm going to fall for, and it's
never the one I fall for." He shot an angry glance at Brian.
"This one is no good. He's bad for business and he's bad
for me. But if I sent him away, I'd probably go looking
for him the next day." He sighed. "Maybe I'll meet
someone else. But you never do when you should."

Axx hit two more joints he figured Kristen favored. Two blanks. He was en route to an establishment known as the Locomotive Lounge when he fell in behind a black-and-white. In the next moment lights were revolving. The cruiser slowed. As Axx passed by he looked over to check out the driver of the car ahead. Nothing was visible. This was a problem a New York cop did not have to deal with: tinted glass on a stopped vehicle in the black of night.

He continued on for thirty yards, then swung over. In the rearview he watched the patrolman approach the car, a hand on his revolver. In a few moments license and registration were passed through an open window. The patrolman returned to his cruiser, then issued the driver a summons.

Just another night on the road. Axx moved off.

He decided he wanted no part of the Locomotive Lounge. Kristen likely would not carry six grams of blow around town as she sampled the local nightlife.

Axx was also hungry for a taste of the day's catch. He was beginning to be sorry this was not Jennifer.

"You hook that bass, boy?"

"He caught me. Then he fell into the boat."

"Like back home."

"I'm beginning to miss it, Boomer. In the city I always knew when something was going down by what happened before it happened—the rumble on the street. I'm not hearing it down here."

"The problem isn't Florida, you're back in bunco is all. It's a different tune."

"This supertrooper has gone tone deaf."

"Maybe you want it too bad. That can make a difference."

"Birkett knew she couldn't stand what he gave her, Boomer. He knew it would kill her."

"One tough case to make."

Brad Axx now knew where the last stop of the evening would be. "I need to pay another visit to the Gulf Shores Yacht Club. But I don't want to go in the front gate."

"One if by land, two if by river?"

"We'll need a boat."

"I told you, I sold my cabin cruiser."

"Find another."

"Boats are noisy, and you can't make them quiet."

"Unless you turn the engine off and row."

"You row into that place under cover of darkness and you are taking a fair chance at ending up underwater. I wouldn't recommend it."

"Kristen was getting her stuff from Birkett Gamble and she was on his boat when he gave her the coke that killed her."

"How do you know that?"

"I was at the marina today and saw the security sheet for that night. She came in with Birkett around eleven-thirty and left twenty minutes later. The next morning she was dead. If I can turn up the same stuff they found on the coffee table in her house, I have a pretty fair case."

"They lock up boats just like they do cars."

"I left the hatch to the head open. All I have to do is get aboard and I can get into it."

"And you don't want to go through the gate?"

"Birkett can't know I've been there. If I find the stuff, I'll leave it. Then I'll get a legal search."

"Okay," said Boomer. "So we need a boat . . ."

★   ★   ★

"You want to borrow it *now?*" The man consulted his watch.

"What's the matter, Harvey, you plan on using it later tonight?"

Harvey shrugged and went around the house to a dock on the river. Bobbing against the current was a rowboat with a tiny outboard motor.

"Am I going to see my boat again, Boomer?"

"That's a very negative point of view, Harvey. Do we look like two people who would go and lose your boat on you?"

"I know you used to be a cop, and this guy probably is one, so the answer to that is yes."

"If this boat is not back tomorrow morning in the same condition in which it is about to leave here, I will personally buy you a new one."

"Well, that sounds all right."

"With his money." Boomer pointed at Axx. "I myself couldn't afford it."

Harvey said, "Now wait just a minute—"

But Axx had already cast off and Boomer got the engine going. It made a tremendous racket.

Boomer shouted, "You *race offshore* in this *machine,* Harvey?"

"If you don't *like* the boat, *leave* the boat!"

They headed downstream. The night sky was regrettably bright. The boat moved at a painfully noisy and leisurely pace.

"How far?" said Axx.

"About a mile."

At a bend in the river Axx saw the looming shapes of large vessels.

"Okay, kid. Make like Johnny Weissmuller."

Axx stood up and stripped off his pants, shirt, and sneakers. He looked along the riverbank.

"Any gators in this part of the river?"

"Yes."

"The least you could do is lie to me."

"Hit him on the nose if he comes at you. They hate that."

"Hit him with what? A hammer?"

"Here," said Boomer, and he tossed Axx a knife with a wooden handle and a serrated blade. Axx had the impression he had seen it before.

"You use this to clean fish!"

"Sure."

"And I am going to stop an alligator with it?"

"Only knife I got, Brooklyn. You forgot to bring one."

Axx slipped his belt out of his pants, buckled it over his BVDs, slid the knife between. Then he eased over the side of the rowboat. He expected the water to be warm. It was not.

"Remember," said Boomer, "aim for the nose."

"What if his jaws are wide open?"

"You got a point there. Maybe it's not the nose you aim for."

"Try to be in the neighborhood when I get back."

Axx pushed off and started swimming. His old man had been a strong swimmer with a smooth stroke. Axx had learned by falling in beside, imitating the father, and trying to stay close. The man usually was too busy keeping his head above financial waters to spend time with his son, who found his own amusements early on, most of them trouble. But every summer they would swim together—Coney Island on Sunday, the Poconos, Myrtle Beach, or Florida on vacation.

But he and the old man had never swum in a river that was home for a creature descended without evolution from prehistory.

He entered the waters of the marina. Light from the docks played across the surface. He kept to the far bank until he spotted Birkett's boat. Then he filled his lungs and dived.

He had the impression he was heading for the front door of the local resident. He surfaced just as his lungs felt about to rupture. He was near a piling and grabbed hold of a rope. The boat before him was Birkett's. He swam to the stern, pulled himself half out by another rope, and looked around.

Nothing was moving. He swung up and over and in, then edged along the gunwale to the bow. He gripped the hatch. Perhaps Birkett had checked it before he left. Axx pulled and the hatch popped open.

Getting through was another question. It appeared larger from below than above. Squeezing in up to his hips, he saw a light go on in the next boat. He swiveled his body violently and slipped through, taking care not to touch down directly below.

He checked every conceivable receptacle. In the stateroom he tapped at walls, looking for a hidden compartment. There was none. Finally he opened the closet and felt along the back wall, where he found the metallic stripping of a piano hinge.

Where there is a hinge, there is usually a door. He turned on a lamp and pushed clothes aside. Recessed above the piano hinge was a brass ring. Axx gripped it and pulled. Down swung a compartment door.

Inside was a small but weighty canvas bag. In it were a dozen Krugerrands. Behind the bag were one-ounce and half-ounce bars, Crédit Suisse. This boat was big enough to travel international waters. Birkett Gamble carried the international currency.

Drug people also liked the color of gold. But these bars were numbered, a drawback. On the other hand someone like Carolyn might take exquisite pleasure by being rewarded in what glitters.

All that was left in the compartment was a nine-millimeter stainless steel Smith & Wesson with a spare clip. No drugs, no works.

Time to hit the water.

The swim back seemed twice as long. There was movement by the reeds along the water. He had the strong impression it was moving toward him. He established a personal best in the thirty-seven-meter freestyle, which brought him to the rowboat.

Like a television announcer covering a big swimming meet, Boomer began questioning him. Like someone just out of the pool after a big race, Axx lay in the boat trying to bring oxygen into his body. Boomer got the message and started the motor.

At the hotel Axx began climbing stairs in a plodding manner.

"Keep your knees loose," said Boomer, "and your glove oiled."

# CHAPTER NINE

"WE have investigated this matter thoroughly, Mr. Axx. Our conclusion is that sole liability rests with the broker at River Woods."

"Would you mind walking me through that step-by-step?"

The president of First Gulf Bank cleared his throat. "Miss McCauley reported inflated sales figures to protect her exclusive representation at River Woods. All certificates are printed by order, complete with the signatures of Mr. Gamble and herself. She merely forwarded fictitious names and addresses to the printer along with the real ones. When the certificates came back, she mailed those going to genuine buyers and kept the phony ones."

"Who approved the order to print certificates?"

"The comptroller."

"Is that a fact?"

Arthur Watt handed him a copy of the print order, which was signed by Walter Ravitt but not by Kristen.

"Mr. Gamble claims he was not involved in any way in the printing and distribution of certificates," said Watt. "He said he found out about the overstated sales figures and bogus certificates after he filed for the acquisition and development loan. When he learned of it, he fired Miss McCauley. I understand she subsequently took her life. Very unfortunate. The complicity of Miss Johns in this scheme has also come to light, which required that she, too, be dismissed."

"Who is your source for all this?"

"We queried both Mr. Gamble and Mr. Ravitt in depth. We are entirely satisfied with what they told us. Their versions corroborate each other."

"Mr. Gamble claims he never saw the certificates or the list of owners?"

"Correct. Miss McCauley sent copies to his office. His secretary filed them away. He relied on Miss McCauley's weekly progress reports, which unfortunately were rather exaggerated."

"Which means he knew nothing was wrong with the sales numbers in his A-and-D application."

"Correct."

"So Mr. Gamble will get his money?"

"We plan to reduce the amount due to improprieties associated with the filing."

"By how much?"

"Four million."

"So you'll give him ten?"

"Correct."

"That should be a lesson to him."

"If we are satisfied with his performance, we may advance the additional four million at a later date."

"When will he get the ten million?"

"Let's see," said the bank president, consulting a desk calendar. "Today is Tuesday. Our loan officer is working up a revised A-and-D proposal along the lines I just described to you. We'll send it registered mail to MFC tomorrow. As soon as they notify us our terms are acceptable, the funds will be advanced. The earliest we could do that is Friday morning. If they don't accept our offer, we start at square one. This is all confidential, of course. I'm divulging it to you because you are a police officer and you went out of your way to advise us about this matter."

"As an investor in River Woods, I hope you are making the right decision."

Arthur Watt leaned back. "We think River Woods is a sound investment. We've thought so all along. The plan of development is excellent. And Birkett Gamble has covered all the bases. Anybody who had to be on board is on board—planning commission, zoning board, town council, environmental people . . . the skids are greased on this one. The man knows what he's doing."

"I agree with you there. But suppose there's some other problem that could deep-six the whole project?"

The bank president folded his hands across his belly. "Then we step in and take over. Hell, it's *our* money he's using to buy and develop River Woods. *We'll* finish the job if we have to."

Axx nodded admiringly. "Birkett is giving you first crack at all new mortgages at River Woods, so that's under your roof, too."

"We'll have a mortgage representative on site. In addition to which we're buying their outstanding paper at a discount. We're going to have River Woods all wrapped up in one package. If we have to pick it up and carry it, we will." He showed the smile of a man who knows he cannot lose.

"Mr. Watt, I'm glad we had this conversation."

"I'd like to thank you once again, Mr. Axx, for bringing this situation to our attention. We'll be keeping close tabs on MFC from here on out to make sure they toe the line. I think they will. They know if they screw up again, they're out and we're in."

"I'll bet you had Birkett Gamble sweating bullets."

"He was rather contrite."

"He ought to be. He's put down a heavy bet. I understand he has a half million or so riding on River Woods."

"I'd say that's a fair estimate—three-seventy on the option, a hundred or so more for the work that's been done so far. If we take over, he loses it all."

"You pitch them high and tight, Mr. Watt."

"You are an investor. As such I am sure you want us to take every precaution to protect your equity."

The president's secretary stuck her head in. "It's Miles Kenyon again. He says he has to talk with you and he'll wait."

Watt glanced annoyedly at the flashing light on his phone. Axx got to his feet. They shook hands. "By the way," said Axx, "I introduced myself to that good-looking redhead across the corridor the other day."

"Ginny."

"I'd like to say hello on the way out, but I don't want to cause her any grief with the boss."

"You're a fast worker, Mr. Axx. Well, by all means go ahead and chitchat. But she can't go to lunch for another hour."

He winked and Axx headed for Ginny's cubicle. The sound of fingers punching at a plastic keyboard told him she was at her machine. He stopped in the doorway. "Is that Brahms or Beethoven?"

"MS/DOS, opus forty-nine."

"You play it with feeling."

"I love my machine."

"I wish I had time for the second movement, but I'm on the job." He removed his wallet and displayed his shield. "I'm doing some work for the bank. Mr. Watt said you could help me."

She moved closer for a better look. He snapped the wallet shut and turned toward the office of the president. He waved. Arthur Watt was on the phone; he nodded and waved back. Axx stepped into the cubicle and out of the line of sight.

"What do you need?" she said.

"The records for MFC Incorporated."

She sat down at the keyboard of her computer. "Which accounts do you want—escrow or working?"

"Both."

She accessed the escrow first. One deposit after another from trusting River Woods investors rolled past. By rough estimate, MFC was holding about one-point-eight million dollars in down-payment money. Because by law these funds couldn't be used to pay River Woods expenses until the buyers took possession of their new homes, this money was kept in a separate escrow account. Expenses were covered by working capital.

"Okay, let's look at the working account."

Axx began at the beginning—a canceled check for a hundred thousand, an early contribution of Janice Kern Gamble that became Birkett's first option payment, now in possession of the retired rancher in Vermont.

A few months later another deposit check of the same amount from the same source, followed by a number of payouts—to architects, road contractors, carpenters, etc.

Then a big number came up: $270,000. It was a deposit made in late October, but not by check. Axx squinted at the screen. The two-seventy came in via electronic transfer from the sending institution. Axx expected this to be a bank in Canada.

What he read was: Account #80685811, Sterling Commonwealth Bank, Nassau, the Bahamas.

Axx was nearly current on the MFC working account when another notation reached out and grabbed him by the eyeballs: instructions to prepare for a funds transfer. From: First Gulf Bank, Gulf Shores, Florida. To: Banco Nacional, Panama City, The Republic of Panama. The transfer was to be made on the fifteenth of the month.

Which was today.

"Thank you, Ginny. You've been very helpful."

"I have?"

"More than you can imagine."

"Great. Do I get a raise?"

"I'll work on it." He noticed a stack of official-looking documents on a long table. On top was a note to one Ms. Krantz from Mr. Ravitt: "As per requested supplementing MFC A&D application." He thumbed through the pile of papers. They were copies of River Woods owner certificates.

"Who is Ms. Krantz?"

"Special assistant in the corporate loan division. I'm dotted line to her."

"Come again?"

"I have to do what she says even though it's not up to her how much money I make."

"There's a lot of that in the army and the NYPD. Is there a private phone I can use?"

She took him to a conference room down the hall. He closed the door and went to a telephone on a small circular table in a corner near a very long table.

"McClellan."

"Tommy me boy."

"Who's this?"

"Your good buddy Brad Axx."

"We're even, Axx."

"I know, Tommy. But now I am going to owe you one."

Thomas D. McClellan was an NYPD bunco detective of eighteen years, adept at ferreting out questionable business dealings, particularly those with an international flavor.

Axx said, "I have an EFT from a numbered account in Nassau."

"Long Island?"

"The Bahamas, Tommy."

"Why don't you find a harder one?"

"I need an ID. I remember you doing some of that when I was in bunco."

"Yeah, we do some of that."

"I need it now."

"I'll make the call. But you're gonna have to pay a visit."

"Where?"

"Fort Lauderdale."

"Can't I phone him?"

"No way he'd go for that. I'll tell him who you are and he'll check you out when you get there."

"Who is he?"

"Danny Ahmed. He runs a thing called Vista Associates out of Fort Lauderdale. International, shall we say, investments. He makes a lot of overnight transfers to places like the Bahamas."

"Will he push on this one?"

"His name came up in an investigation not too long ago. He is worried about it. I told him not to be."

"Call him now."

"Where are you?"

Axx gave him the number showing on the telephone, hung up, waited. Fifteen minutes later, "Get on your horse and ride, cowboy."

He took Alligator Alley across. His father had gone this route during one of their aimless vacation forays. Axx remembered the monotonous landscape unreeling like an endless nightmare, relieved only by the crunching sound the tires made passing over various forms of wildlife, chief among them, snakes.

"Lord, do not let me break down now," the old man would incant.

Nothing much had changed along the Everglades Parkway—swampland to the horizon.

Traffic was light and Axx barreled. He was flagged down once, identified himself as on official police business, and roared on. His memory of Fort Lauderdale was vague, but on arrival he recalled the skyline being a lot lower. In the lobby of an oceanside high rise he found a listing for Vista Associates. He went up to the twelfth floor and through a door into a peach-and-cream waiting room where nobody was waiting.

"Mr. Axx?" said the receptionist. "Go right in."

Danny Ahmed was a small man with a large belly who sat in a chair so big he looked like a bearded child. Various electronic apparatuses covered his desk. These included three telephones, into one of which he was speaking.

"Yes, tomorrow, I said. *Tomorrow!*" He slammed the phone down and looked at his visitor. "That guy wouldn't know what to do with an ax handle. He'd stand there scratching his head and tell you, 'I think there's supposed

to be something sharp and shiny on it, but I'm not sure.' "
The narrow blinds threw thin bars of lights across the
dwarfish body. "You are a colleague of Mr. McClellan?"

"True blue."

"He said you require my assistance."

Axx fed him the account number and the name of the
bank in Nassau. Ahmed consulted a personal directory.
Stubby fingers punched out the number with the deft
precision of one who spends the greater part of each day
patronizing telecommunications companies.

"Mr. Wellington, please." A pause, and then, with
indisputable charm, "Hello, Richard!" They chatted about
the weather, after which Ahmed made his request. A
silence of several minutes ensued, during which time
everybody in the room regarded the view. "Yes . . . yes
. . . thank you, Richard. Soon, probably next week. Good-
bye." To Axx he said, "This is a construction account, for
Island Works Limited."

"I need the name of a human being."

"I have the president but it's a DBA. One John D.
Jones."

" 'Doing Business As' isn't good enough."

Danny Ahmed shrugged. "Whoever opened this account did it the right way. It's going to take more than a
phone call to get what you need."

"Tommy McClellan said I could count on you."

"I'm sure he would be the first to admit these matters
take time, Mr. Axx. The reason for having a numbered
offshore account, you see, is to make it very difficult for
anyone to identify the owner."

"Mr. McClellan thinks I owe him a favor. He is going
to be very disappointed when I tell him I don't."

Ahmed looked crestfallen. "I wish there was something
I could tell you, Mr. Axx."

"You can."

Danny Ahmed leaned forward expectantly.

"Where's the nearest airport?"

The major carriers had no flights to Tallahassee scheduled for when Axx wished to depart, which was at once. He decided to try one of the regional airlines. The one he found was extremely regional.

The props seemed to generate as much noise inside as out. There were two other passengers. One was a balding man in a beige suit who carried a shiny briefcase, sat near the wing, and kept looking out the window at the engine as if expecting, perhaps hoping, it would fail before departing the gate. The other passenger was an emaciated girl oblivious to all. She looked like a mule who had prepared for the flight by taking a liberal dose of the product she was packing.

Axx placed a large envelope on the seat beside him and pressed the recline button on his armrest.

The captain welcomed everybody aboard Sunshine Express 101 bound for . . . uh, Tallahassee. He further announced the flight attendant couldn't make it this time out. The copilot came lumbering back into the cabin to run a preflight check and try to look like he gave a hey. He maneuvered toward Axx's seat, which was at the very rear of the plane, Axx having an idea this was the safest location, as if he were in a Times Square movie theater. "Buckle up, babe," the copilot advised, "we're gonna get this bastard off the ground in about two minutes."

They did, too. The issue was in doubt until that last, abrupt lift. Then she leveled off and settled into what for Axx resembled the spin cycle of a coin-op in the Suds Your Duds emporium over on Ninth Avenue.

About halfway to Tallahassee the cockpit door popped open to reveal an indistinct but intense exchange of words among the flight crew. This was followed by the sound of breaking glass. The door was pulled shut.

To take his mind off this, Axx fixed on the approval by First Gulf of Birkett Gamble's A-and-D loan. The story purchased by Arthur Watt was one Brad Axx would not read to a preschooler. The bank was looking for a reason to stay in the deal, and Birkett gave them one: I fired my brokers for fraud.

Then there was the matter of Walter Ravitt. He claimed to know slightly more than nothing about River Woods buyer certificates—hearsay from Kristen on slowed sales, toss-off remarks by Birkett Gamble about funny A-and-D numbers. But that was the comptroller's signature on the certificate print order Arthur Watt had offered as Exhibit A exonerating Birkett. Which meant Ravitt could have kept a running count on sales figures all along. And that was the comptroller's cover letter on the stack of certificate copies sent to the bank in support of the A-and-D application. Meaning he likely had access to the originals, and perhaps the complete list of River Woods buyers.

But why turn Axx to any of this? Why the sweaty palms, the coy hints? If Axx were comptroller, he would be stonewalling for all he was worth. And if Walter Ravitt had a list of certificate holders, which he probably did, why did Axx have to do a B&E on the office of Birkett Gamble to get a copy?

Sunshine Express Flight 101 touched down on schedule at Tallahassee airport, then touched down again, once more, and a final time. They taxied up to what looked like an open field, where they rested in relative peace until someone began working on the departure door from the outside. Axx expected to climb down a painter's ladder to what in no way would resemble tarmac. He hoped it wasn't quicksand.

The door opened, at which time the copilot expressed his appreciation for the patronage of his passengers: "Thanks a lot. Have fun if you can find it."

Michael A. Edwards squatted and squinted. Then he stood and turned sideways, hunching a bit before swinging his arms in a motion intended to be pendulumlike. In execution this was a jerk and a push, which caused him to slide by on the high side.

He didn't care. It was a beautiful day and the ninth green of the Long Acres Country Club was far removed from the office of the state attorney. The moment was made more enjoyable by his partner missing a two-foot gimme. The caddies hefted their bags and trundled toward the tenth tee. The golfers headed for the clubhouse.

When they were seated at a table overlooking the burnt-out fairways, Edwards's partner, a dentist who wore blue-and-white golf shoes with pink slacks, said, "What steams me is, I spent a hundred bucks on lessons this week. Geez, if we don't get some rain, this course will play like the highway."

"How do we stand, Harry?"

The dentist removed a card and pencil from his pocket and began adding. "You're three up. . . ."

"Tell you what," said Edwards. "Double the bet, start even on the back nine."

Harry grinned. "Mike, baby, I am now going to demonstrate what a hundred dollars of lessons can do for a man's golf game."

Next to the pro shop stood a man in white boat pants,

a khaki shirt, and dirty sneakers. He was certainly not a
member. His hands were shoved deep in his pockets and
he was looking at Michael Edwards. A manila envelope
was in the crook of one arm.

"How about another round before I take you to the
cleaners?" said Harry the dentist.

They ordered and soon their drinks were placed in front
of them by the man with the manila envelope. He then
took a seat at their table.

"Who are you supposed to be?" said Harry.

Axx flashed his NYPD shield. "Your caddy is under
arrest."

"What?"

"Possession of narcotics. We are confiscating your golf
bag. Officer Carmichael is outside. He has a few questions
for you."

The dentist looked dazedly at his golf partner, who
said, "Go ahead, Harry. I'll be down later to bail you
out." Edwards watched the unsteady exit of his playing
partner. "He won't be able to drop a three-inch putt after
this." He turned to Axx. "You look like a cop all right,
but the shields here are silver."

"This one comes from New York."

"A far piece."

"The problem is local."

"How did you find me?"

"Your secretary will fill you in tomorrow. Something
about your brother out at the airport just in from France."

"I don't have a brother."

"We know that but she doesn't."

"What is the problem you are bringing to me, sir?"

"The problem is Mr. Keye."

"Jimmy? One of my best people."

"I gave him a case. He put it back on the elevator and pushed the down button."

"What case?"

"Real estate fraud."

"We see a lot of that."

"Now it's a case of murder." Axx unclasped the envelope, from which he extracted the report of the county medical examiner and the list of phony River Woods certificate holders.

"Why are you showing me this autopsy report?"

"She was a broker who got hooked up with a hustler from Toronto. She found out he was falsifying sales figures to get A-and-D money."

"Does the bank know this?"

"The bank needs the business. They are also taking heat from the locals to finance the project because of all the good things it brings. Like paychecks and tax revenue and free parks. If you pushed their face in it, they would probably ask you for a fork."

"And this broker got killed over these fraudulent certificates?"

"Ten big ones from the A-and-D are going into the Gulf Shores account of the Toronto bad guy on Friday. He has a numbered one in Panama. It's a bust-out from day one. It's why he came down here. He incorporated this real estate promotion with one intention—to walk with the assets and bankrupt the company."

"How do you know that?"

"He left instructions with both banks to get ready for an EFT on the fifteenth."

"That is today."

"His loan got delayed because of some snowbird cop, but the transfer order is still good. It will happen Friday morning."

"How do I get a murder case out of this?"

"The broker was no dummy. She learned about the scam. Maybe she threatened to blow it. Maybe she wanted a piece of it. Either way, she dealt herself into the wrong game."

"Says here she died of an overdose of cocaine."

Axx presented his thoughts on this. The state attorney said, "What did this guy do, shove pure grade up her nose and make her inhale it? This report shows some deterioration of the nasal cavity. She was a user."

"Are you telling me there is no precedent for prosecuting someone who supplies drugs to a user who dies from them? And in this case the death was intentional. That is murder."

The state attorney tossed the papers on the table. "You went to a lot of trouble to find me."

"I am almost finished. Mr. Big had two payments to make on the property he is using to run the scam—a hundred when he took the option last June, two-seventy more six months later, in November. The first hundred came from his new bride. He put up the two-seventy, which came from guess where? A numbered Nassau account. That money has got to be dirty, which brings up other possibilities in the way of litigation."

"What should I do about all this?"

"Get a court order freezing all assets of his company so he can't send a seashell out of the country. This has to happen by Thursday because he's packing his sack and he's a gone Jack the next day. But he is going nowhere without that geld."

"That's all?"

"For now."

"Well, let's take it point by point. I like to be logical,

Axx. On the certificate fraud—small potatoes, just another tall-talking, slick-dicking son of a bitch trying to put some shine on his deal. That's fraud all right, but it's the bank's problem. If they don't want it, neither do I."

He took a slow sip from his drink. "Second, the embezzlement. International bank accounts are opened every day of the week down here. Maybe your man shoots the juice down to Panama. In which case that idiot bank in Gulf Shores gets what it deserves"

Axx said, "He took in about one-point-eight million from actual buyers, most of them working people. That goes with him."

"Which, after all this is perpetrated, would probably help me get a true bill out of a grand jury if I was interested, but I won't be."

"Why is that?"

"I only try to play a fish I can really set the hook into. This boy is going to throw anything you try to catch him with. *That's* his scam. I'll be busting my butt until the year two thousand making a case on this guy and getting him into court. For what? One-point-eight million belonging to a handful of small-time investors? I wouldn't waste bait on this guy."

Harry the dentist came bustling up. "My goddamn caddy is over at the tenth tee cleaning my clubs and there's nobody named Carmichael waiting outside to talk to me."

"Sit down and finish your drink, Harry," said the state attorney. "Now I won't have to bail you out." He looked at Axx. "Where were we? Ah yes, third, the murder that isn't. The local constable closed the case and you come to me so I can throw a downfield block or two while you run the ball. Well, maybe they work that way where you come from, but this sure isn't New York, Mr. Axx, it surely isn't." To his golfing partner he said, "Double the stakes, Harry?"

"Yeah, right. Who is this guy?"

"Nobody, Harry. He's just visiting from up north."

"One wise-ass snowbird . . ."

Axx watched through the window as they ambled in many-pasteled splendor toward the tenth tee. In addition to the unpleasant events that had transpired here, he now faced the prospect of again paying good money to push the outside of the envelope in the friendly skies of Sunshine Express.

Axx got lucky. He caught a commuter flight back to Kingston on an airline that had previously entered the jet age.

When he arrived at Boomer's, the hood of the jeep was open and a burly back was bent over the engine. As Axx approached he heard unkind words issue forth.

"What's the problem here?"

Boomer raised a grease-stained face. "The alternator crapped out. I don't like to buy alternators. I don't appreciate the price."

He slammed the hood in place and said to the jeep, "You can just sit there until I get good and ready," and to Axx, "Somebody called looking for you."

"Who?"

"Irishman by the name of Ahmed."

"Did he leave a message?"

"Wouldn't do it. Had to talk with you yourself. Ellie has the number."

Axx hustled inside and got on the phone. Danny Ahmed answered. "I have made further efforts in your regard, Mr. Axx."

"And?"

"I will be in Nassau on business next Tuesday. I will be able to look into this matter personally the next day. I should have something for you by the end of the week."

"I'll be waiting for your call, Danny."

Boomer came in as he hung up. "Get cleaned up, Pop. Then pack a bag."

"What for?"

"I've got business. I need somebody to watch my back."

"Where?"

"The Bahamas."

"Beats Chicagoland."

$\bigtriangledown$

# CHAPTER TEN

$\mathbf{A}$xx had wanted to honeymoon in Nassau. A travel agent who was a sister of a vice detective said she would love to take the booking, but the Caribbean climate in August was more suitable for people *ending* marriages. So they went to Niagara Falls, Canadian side, which was fine with Marcia; she had never been out of the state.

"Do I need a passport?" Axx said to Boomer.

"Just proof of citizenship. I don't suppose you have your birth certificate with you?"

"I forgot it."

"Voter registration card?"

"Next question."

They made the last flight out of Kingston that evening to Miami, where they found a customs officer and explained their business. Soon Axx was carrying a white immigration card and sitting in a window seat sipping a Bahama Mama.

They were through Nassau International Airport in two minutes. "They don't care what you bring in," said Boomer. "Outgoing is something else again."

Boomer stopped at a pay phone and made a call. Then they went out front and got in a cab. The driver was sitting on the right side of the car. Boomer said, "The Sand and Surf."

The driver said nothing and in a few moments they were proceeding along the left side of the road. The disorienting effect was enhanced by the speed at which they were traveling.

"Slow down," said Boomer.

"I drive, you ride."

"Your meter isn't on."

"Meter broken, don't worry 'bout it."

"How much to the hotel?"

"Don't worry 'bout it."

Axx glimpsed a beach under moonlight before they made a sharp right and began climbing a hill. At the top they made a right, another left, and slid to a halt in front of a weathered sign advertising the Sand and Surf Hotel. In the darkness Axx could see the low-profile outline of a stone building with small windows.

It seemed they would be staying the night in the local prison.

The driver now spoke. "Thirty dollar."

With this a large black face appeared at the window on the other side. "Boomer!"

"E!"

"Thirty dollar," repeated the driver.

The black face peering in looked at the meter and frowned. A bill was tossed into the lap of the driver. "Now off with you before I turn you in."

The taxi departed behind a cloud of dust.

"He claimed his meter was busted," said Boomer.

"There was nothing wrong with his meter. Coming in late he hoped you'd be too tired to argue."

Ellis turned out to be a former UCLA fullback and

LAPD lieutenant who owned a part interest in the Sand and Surf with his Bahamian wife. This establishment was located only a short distance from the glitzy resort hotels but nevertheless had no sand or surf to brag about.

"Name sounds nice," said Ellis, "and I can get you a good rental deal on a car so you can get to the beach if you want."

"We're strictly business this time over," said Boomer. "But that's for tomorrow."

The night was cool and they sat in the courtyard with a round of drinks that had strange names and all seemed to be made with rum.

"They make the stuff on the other end of the island," said Ellis. "As far as local manufacturing goes, that's about it. The rest of what we sell is sun, sand, and surf—and games of chance."

Axx viewed the ocean the next morning on the way to town. It was green and white.

"That's because it's shallow," said Boomer. "Bahamas is Portuguese for shallow waters. But it's deep enough to drown in. If you thought Florida was different, get ready."

The cab deposited them in front of a marina. At the end of a long dock was a small square office.

"Looks like Island Works Limited is working off one of these yachts," said Axx.

"Nice work if you can get it."

Under a tree by the road a man was roasting food on a hibachi. "Start de day right, mon. Have yourself some of dis."

Axx stepped up and studied what looked like shrimp but wasn't.

"Fritters, mon."

"Conch meat," said Boomer.

"What's a conch?"

"Come out of a big seashell," said the man. "Best eating aroun'. You can go spend all your money in dose fancy rest-aurants but you won't find nothin' better to eat than right here."

Axx was game—he had become used to eating seafood first thing in the morning. But breakfast was already history.

"See you at lunchtime."

They started into the marina, which was home for a number of impressive craft. Tied up among these were two low boats that appeared to have been carved out of large tree trunks. In the bow of each was a pile of nets.

The marina office was the quarters of the dockmaster, who they found completing a sale to one of the more affluent boat owners.

"I'm looking for Marina Way," said Axx.

"You were on it."

They went back out to the dock, on which in front of each boat was painted a number. Before a sleek sport fisher was 32. They followed the numbers—22, 16, 10 . . . and were almost at roadside again when they located 4 Marina Way. They looked down at the two hand-carved fishing boats.

"Lookin' for me, boss?"

It was the fritter salesman.

"Is this Four Marina Way?" said Axx.

"You got it."

"And you, sir, must be John D. Jones, sole proprietor of Island Works Limited."

The man's gap-toothed smile disappeared. He turned back to his hibachi.

"I think we ought to go pay a visit to Sterling Commonwealth," Axx said to Boomer.

They walked through what Axx took to be downtown,
a collection of tourist shops along a shady thoroughfare,
toward the end of which was the bank. Its front was
pinkish marble and glass. Boomer posted himself outside.
Inside, Axx stopped at the first teller.

"Mr. Wellington, please."

He was directed to an office at the rear of the bank. On
the wall next to the door was a plate reading, R.E. WEL-
LINGTON, VICE-PRESIDENT. A woman was posted at a desk
out front. Axx heard conversation from inside the office
and went past the woman.

"Excuse me!" she said.

"Of course."

Mr. Wellington was on the telly. He looked at Axx and
then his secretary and then back at Axx. In the clipped
accent of his homeland, he said, "I have a bloody visitor.
Noon, then. Yes, good-bye."

Before the secretary could speak, Axx said, "I'm an
acquaintance of Danny Ahmed."

Wellington was extremely fair with thick blond hair. He
waved his secretary away. "I talked with Danny just yesterday."

"I was sitting in his office at the time."

"So you were the inspiration for his call."

"I'm a police officer from New York. He owed a friend
of mine a favor. I'm working a case."

Milk white hands lifted a pipe from an ashtray. A safety
match was removed from a silver-plated box on the desk.
"I am particular about using wooden matches. They provide an even, consistent light. I feel everything should be
done in the proper manner. Otherwise there are consequences, whether you are ignorant of them or not."
Smoke billowed up. He flicked the match into the silver

ashtray. "Danny failed to inform me you would be visiting our lovely isle."

Axx reached over and lifted the telephone handset. "Call him."

Wellington began to do so, then hung up. "Not necessary. You see, I have nothing more for you."

"The case I am investigating involves bank fraud."

"Do you have any idea how many accounts are opened on this island for the express purpose of sheltering funds obtained by fraud or otherwise illegal methods?"

"The case also has a murder attached to it. That is what I am after."

"And you want me to tell you whodunit?"

"I want you to tell me who belongs to a DBA for Island Works Limited, which is headquartered in a conch boat at a marina a few blocks away."

"Fellow selling fritters by the road?"

"That's him."

The man chuckled. "You were looking at one of the largest conglomerates in the western hemisphere. He hasn't the foggiest notion, of course. He gets a small fee that he can't afford to live without."

"And who pays him that?"

"We do, among others. For our clients."

"And Island Works Limited is one of them."

"That's what I told Danny."

"You also gave him a DBA, John D. Jones. I need to know just who that is."

"I do not possess that information."

"Mr. Ahmed seems to think you do. He was going to check into it when he visited here next week."

"The account did not originate here."

"Why did he call you?"

"You gave him our name and the account number. It's a DBA, and in some cases I might know the name behind the name, but in this case I don't. We merely expedited the paperwork, which was sent back to the party about whom you are inquiring through the intermediary. You see, the client didn't deal directly with us."

"Who, then?"

"The government."

Axx watched what he was reaching for suddenly recede. "That's not a who, that's a what."

"Quite right. OED, to be precise."

"Which is?"

"Office of Economic Development. We were simply ordered to provide the necessary repository for a transfer of funds associated with a government construction project."

"For Island Works Limited of Four Marina Way and one John D. Jones?"

"That is what the order said, that is what we did."

"Who in OED gave you this order?"

Wellington shouted, "Elizabeth!"

The secretary appeared at his desk. "That account I perused late yesterday, is it refiled yet?"

"Myrna has it."

"Please bring it."

When the file was handed to him, he flipped through it quickly and removed a sheet of paper. "This is the order," he said, handing it to Axx. "You tell me who gave it to us."

There were all manner of official insignia, but nowhere an official title or signature.

Wellington said, "It has the proper stamp of approval, which is good enough for us."

Outside, Boomer was chatting with a local constable, outfitted in black pants, white jacket, and white helmet, all of which in this climate could serve as humane punishment for minor offenses.

"How did we do, Brooklyn?"

Axx was thumbing through a tour guide. "Let's go sight-seeing."

They climbed stone steps to a shuttered two-story building flanked by palms. A plaque identified it as the General Administrative Offices, which matched up with the description in Axx's guide. Inside the lobby they found a directory of official agencies that sent them to the second floor, Room 212.

They knocked and entered. A young man whose skin glowed blue black against the white of his shirt looked up briefly, then went back to what he was doing, which involved writing on a piece of paper. An overhead fan turned lazily.

"Is this the Office of Economic Development?" said Axx.

"Yes." The man continued writing.

Axx said to Boomer, "I think he was trained by Jimmy Keye."

This got Axx some attention; the clerk put down his pen. "What is your business here?"

"I would like to discuss economic development with someone."

"Development of what?"

"My partner and I are in the construction business in Florida. We want to expand our horizons."

The man went back to his chores. "There are strenuous restrictions and regulations on foreign-owned businesses. It is a very lengthy procedure."

"How long would it take?"

"Years."

"My partner is getting along, but I'm willing to give it a shot. Who do we need to talk to first?"

A number of official-looking forms were slapped down on the counter. "You need to fill these out first."

"And then?"

"They will be processed with all the others."

"Fine," said Axx. "But tell me, could we speed things up a bit?"

"How do you mean?"

"I mean, who do we need to talk to and when can we talk to him?"

"The minister is out of the office today."

"Who is the minister?"

"Mr. Camoon."

"When will he return?"

"Not today."

"How about an appointment for tomorrow?"

"He doesn't like to come to the office. People always want to talk to him."

They were at the door when the man behind the counter said, "You forgot your forms."

Ellis grinned. "Ah yes, Robert Camoon. He is a sly one."

"He's a minister in the government, we are told."

"He is a gofer in the government, I am telling you. The ministers here, they get shuffled in, out, around. It's not much of a job, you see. The pay is lousy. But they make it up elsewhere."

Axx said, "He made some of it up by handling a financial matter on behalf of a client stateside."

"Yes, that is common."

"I need to know more about that transaction. I need to know who it was in behalf of."

"That will be difficult."

"Tell us about Robert Camoon," said Boomer.

"He does very well for a minister. He has many friends who are wealthy. He is seen everywhere. He appears not to work."

"We found that out firsthand."

"Where does he like to be seen?" said Axx.

"Yacht clubs, the best restaurants, discos, the casino."

Axx looked at Boomer and vice versa. "He is a gambling man," said Boomer.

"Not much of one. But they say he makes money at it."

"Where does he play?"

"He's got to be careful in the casino. He can't be seen betting too much."

"Back room?" said Axx.

"Off premises."

"Where do we find him?" said Boomer.

"The Bali Club is the first place I'd look."

"Where's that?"

"Not far from the marina."

"Could you point out Mr. Camoon to us?" said Axx.

"Sure."

"We are going to need some serious jack," said Boomer.

"How much?" asked Ellis.

"Two thousand."

"I can give you fifteen hundred from the safe."

"I am also going to need some iron."

"I've got a Smith and Wesson forty-four."

"That will be fine."

Soon they were in two cabs taking separate routes to

the Bali Club. The doorman was tipped generously by Boomer, who arrived first, then Axx, who got out of a cab with Ellis. The doorman looked hard at Ellis.

"Do you know that guy?" said Axx.

"They don't like locals in the casinos."

"But Camoon comes here."

"He is a minister. That can be useful."

The interior was plush and hushed. A room to the side housed the slots. It was jammed. They went out onto the floor, which was not as congested.

"I'll be at the bar," Axx said to Ellis. "If you find Camoon, swing by me and I'll follow. Then either stand or sit next to him and nod. After that, split, we'll take it."

Mr. Camoon was at a blackjack table. Axx sat down at his side, Boomer two seats away, the chair in the middle remained empty.

"Gentlemen," said the dealer, pleased to see more action arrive.

Boomer played Loud Foreigner, Axx played Drunk Foreigner. They both played loose, taking a hit when they should fold, and conversely. They both lost. Mr. Camoon also lost, but seemed not to mind. Finally Boomer said, "I don't like this place. I don't like blackjack."

Robert Camoon smiled. "What type of game do you prefer, sir?"

"Five-card stud."

Axx broke in. "Nah, seven-card is the game."

"Five, I'm telling you!" said Boomer. "But not in a joint like this!" He looked up at the ceiling. "I feel like a guppy in a fishbowl." He turned to Camoon. "Can I buy ya a drink?"

"I would feel slighted if you would not allow me the pleasure. I, too, dislike institutionalized gambling."

"How about you, buddy?" Boomer said to Axx. "You're from the states, ain'tcha?"

"Sure am."

They left the dealer with a double deck of cards and one player to deal to, a plump woman who regarded him as if he was about to assault her. She quickly slid off her chair and bustled away.

After one round at the bar, Camoon said, "If you gentlemen are agreeable, I know of a very private game I think you would find most interesting. We are playing tonight."

"Where is that?"

"He is an industrialist from your country who keeps a home on the island, which he visits on occasion. It overlooks the ocean."

"Hey, that sounds **great!**" said Boomer.

"I don't know," said Axx. "How far is this place?"

"Just a few miles. It is very safe, I assure you. I would not venture there if it were not. And I should tell you, he thinks he is a good card player but he is not. I have seen him lose a great deal of money. But then, money is nothing to him."

"Sounds like somebody I should meet!" said Boomer. "What do you say, buddy?"

"Okay," said Axx. "Let's go."

Soon they were reclining in a limousine racing at alarming speed along the waterfront. They turned down a steep driveway that curved around and about. The limo stopped in front of a large house near which the sea could be heard lapping against rocks below. The game room was wood-paneled and had its own bar.

Three men were at the bar. Mr. Walsh, whose residence this was, welcomed them heartily. He was gray-haired and wore evening clothes. He said he was from Pittsburgh, retired from the steel industry. The remaining two were considerably younger and dressed in suits. Mr. Michaud was compact and cordial and spoke with a French accent. Mr. Fenton, tall and thin, with a hooked nose and sharp black eyes, was introduced as a statesider. He seemed less enthusiastic about their presence.

The poker table was circular and fitted with dark green felt. Michaud reached for the cards. Fenton sat to his left, to the right was Walsh, and to his right, Robert Camoon. Axx and Boomer were across from them.

As Michaud began dealing, Walsh, whose game it was, said, "Gentlemen, the deal is courtesy of the house. I am reimbursing Mr. Michaud for his services. This is customary in private games of this type, as I am sure you are aware."

"Of course," said Boomer, tight-lipped.

"Fine with me," Axx said reluctantly.

Axx had hoped to take all present, and the minister in particular, for a large sum of money, which would buy the name he needed. That all changed with the first deal.

The deck was shaved, face cards and aces.

Axx let a jack fall to the floor so he could examine it further. The corners were trimmed evenly and smoothly. It was first-rate paperwork, unnoticeable to the pigeons they were impersonating. Axx began looking for the shill. Only Walsh did not bother to cover his hole card the moment it was dealt to him. Michaud's hands were busy but did not show a mechanic's grip.

A quick tally of the team's chips told Axx that he and Boomer had twelve hundred left between them. Boomer won a hand, Axx a couple. He tried to act like he was thrilled by this. The minister's luck was poor and remained so. Likewise the distinguished-looking Walsh.

The dealer began to fare a little better. Fenton, much better.

Boomer now sat with two jacks showing and one card to be dealt. "Two hundred." Everybody in attendance was beat on the board and folded, except Fenton, who showed six high. The next card dealt him was a king. Boomer drew a five.

"Two hundred," Boomer said to the hawk-faced man.

"And two more." Fenton casually slid four hundred in chips into the middle of the table. Boomer met that but had nothing in the hole. Fenton turned up the second king.

"You're a tough man to beat, Mr. Fenton," said Boomer.

Four hands later, Axx had queen high out of three showing. He also had a lady in the hole. "Three hundred." The minister and Fenton stayed in. Axx had been counting cards. Two aces were already dead.

Fenton pulled an ace, then turned over a second. Fenton was the shill. Michaud was base dealer, and a good one.

The minister's job was to steer lambs to this slaughter, while Walsh apparently was either a terminal pigeon or took a percentage for supplying the premises.

"Where in the States are you from, Mr. Fenton?" said Boomer, with the lift of an eyebrow acknowledging to Axx that he saw it, too.

"Oklahoma."

"Oil and gas?"

"A working well here and there."

"You must hit a lot of gushers."

"I get my share."

"I bet you do."

Axx lost again. He grabbed at his drink, spilling some of it on himself. Since the deal did not rotate, there was only one way to beat this grift and he would have to do it now. He pushed himself up, drink in hand. "This here seat is unlucky! Mr. Walsh, would be kind enough to switch with me, sir?"

"Well, I—"

But Axx was already staggering around to the other side of the table, and Walsh assented. Axx now sat at the right of the dealer, Michaud. He glanced to the other side of Michaud, at Fenton, who appeared unconcerned.

The shaved cards had a slight sheen visible up close. Axx was now in position to read every hole card just before it was dealt, particularly the hole card of Mr. Fenton. He saw Boomer lean back in relief.

On the second hand Boomer sat with a nine showing, Axx an eight. Fenton was king high. His hole card was not shaved.

The bet came to Axx. He looked at Boomer, who sniffled. Boomer had the second nine in the hole. "I raise four hundred," said Axx.

The dealer folded. Fenton said, "I'm in."

When the bet came to Boomer, he said, "Five more."

Inasmuch as Axx was eight high and his initial bet was a signal to Boomer to jump in feetfirst, he folded. Fenton pushed five hundred into the pot, figuring Boomer for a bluff. Then he turned up a ten. Boomer slowly showed a second nine.

In three hours Boomer accumulated chips amounting to fourteen thousand dollars, Axx a pile worth another eight.

Finally Axx said, "Well, gentlemen, I think it is time to turn out the lights on this charade."

"What do you mean, sir?" said Walsh, offended.

"I mean, sir, I am not sure what your role here tonight

is, but Mr. Michaud is middle-dealing a shaved deck to
Mr. Fenton."

"Are you calling me a cheat?" said Fenton, aggrieved.

"I am calling you a second-rate worker not slick enough
to spot a couple of laymen who are partners."

"Partners?" said the minister.

"Shut up, you chump!" Fenton snapped. "Nobody
vouched for these guys, did they, Robert? You met them
at the casino and they acted like a couple of square johns,
so you brought them here." He turned to Axx. "Are you
going to tell us why you are blowing your hustle?"

"I don't want your money," said Axx. With this,
Boomer emitted a sharp cough.

"What *do* you want?"

"Information."

Fenton laughed. "What information do I have that you
want?"

"You don't. He does." Axx jerked his thumb at Robert
Camoon. "And if he comes across, you can keep your
twenty-two K, minus five. If he does not, you not only
lose the geld but Mr. Camoon's activities here will be
made known to his employers, the management of the
Bali casino, and anybody else around town I think might
be interested. I am going to put a sign on his back."

"What information could you possibly want from me?"
said Camoon.

"The name of the DBA in a numbered account for
Island Works Limited. I want him."

"I am sure I have no idea what you are talking about. I
am an employee of the government serving as liaison with
the private sector."

Boomer said, "That goes over like a turd in a toilet."

Walsh pushed his chair back. "Robert, you and these

men have some personal business to discuss." He began to leave the room with the dealer and Fenton.

"All right, yes, all right," Camoon said. "Come by my office tomorrow and I will give you the name."

"I want it tonight."

"I cannot do that. There is security at the building. I am never there at this hour. It would be noticed by my superiors."

"Think of an excuse."

"Please be reasonable. I will have it for you tomorrow."

"He said he'd give you what you want," said Fenton. "Now haul your ass out of here."

Axx plunked the Colt .357 down on the table. Robert Camoon jumped. "When I leave here with my partner and your twenty-two thousand dollars, I want we should all be friends."

Another man stepped into the room from a side door. He had a hand inside his jacket. Axx snatched up the .357 at about the same time Walsh shouted "No!" in a tone that was hard and commanding. It was his game, all right. The man let his hand drop. Walsh turned to Axx. "You will have safe passage, but you should prepare to leave."

It was two in the morning when they arrived back at the Sand and Surf Hotel carrying two designer briefcases supplied by the accommodating Mr. Walsh.

Ellis was waiting. "Did the minister take the bait?"

"He was steering to a rigged game," said Boomer. "The barracuda, a Mr. Fenton from Oklahoma, he claims. He thought he had a couple of veal cutlets, but he was the one who got fried."

They opened the briefcases.

"Damn!" breathed Ellis. "How much is that?"

"Twenty-two," said Axx.

"Better open the safe, E," said Boomer.

They lined the top shelf with stacks, four of which Axx put below. "These belong to the house," he told Ellis.

"Wait a minute, I gave you fifteen hundred."

"Your fifteen, plus thirty-five. A man should make a fair return on his investment."

"I guess that fixes the swimming pool. But this isn't Vegas. You better send your eyeballs around the corner ahead of you until you leave the country. Your Mr. Walsh is connected."

"The money isn't going out with us," said Axx.

"Huh?"

"We're going to spend it," said Boomer.

"How long are you staying?"

"We leave tomorrow."

"Okay, that's it." Ellis shut the safe. "If you boys are through doing whatever you are doing until tomorrow, I am going to bed."

"Good night," said Axx.

"Pleasant dreams," said Boomer.

"You're staying up?"

Boomer said, "Getting rid of this much money takes some planning." Ellis shook his head and trudged out. "Well, Brooklyn," said Boomer, "tell me. How are we going to get off this island alive?"

They were at the Office of Economic Development at 9:30 the next morning. To the clerk Axx said, "Mr. Camoon, please."

"Do you have an appointment?"

"He's expecting us."

"Oh?"

"Be a good fellow and tell him he has visitors."

The clerk showed a lot of teeth. "He's not here."

They had a noon flight to Miami. "When will he be in?" said Axx.

"I'm sure I don't know." The clerk went back to his chores.

"Camoon is going to job us," said Boomer.

"That would cost his friends a lot of money and Mr. Camoon a great deal of grief."

They sat. The minister appeared at ten. When they were in his office, he said, "I did not want to deviate from routine."

Each of them opened the briefcase he was carrying, displayed its contents, then snapped it shut. "Island Works Limited," said Axx. "Give . . ."

Camoon rummaged through a drawer in his desk. "Just a minute." He got up and went out.

"I don't think I like this," said Boomer.

"I hate it."

When the minister reappeared, he was accompanied by two policemen.

"Gentlemen," said Robert Camoon, "these men are here to escort you."

"Where are we going?" said Axx.

"They wish to speak with you about your crime."

"What crime is that?" said Boomer.

"Attempted bribery of a public official. It is a very serious offense here."

Axx flipped the snaps on one of the briefcases and opened it. It was jammed with stacks bound by rubber bands. He slipped the top bill from one stack. The paper below it showed white.

Boomer leaned close to the minister. "You obviously are not accustomed to dealing in cash, sir. Always see the money—all of it."

To the police officers Camoon said, "You are dismissed." They went out and Robert Camoon sat down at his desk.

"Let's begin again," said Axx. "Island Works Limited . . ."

The minister took pen in hand and scrawled on a piece of paper, which he pushed across the desk. On it was written, "Wilbur Roos."

"Who is Wilbur Roos?" said Axx.

"You wanted a name, you have a name."

"I need a place."

"Florida."

"Florida is a big place."

"That is all you will get from me. It should be enough for two such enterprising individuals."

Axx crumpled the paper. They started out.

"Do not expect to get off this island with our money," said the minister.

"We don't have it anymore," said Axx.

"What?"

Boomer said, "By this he means it is no longer in our possession."

"I should warn you—"

"You need to go to the bank, Mr. Camoon," said Axx.

"I beg your pardon?"

"You need to go to the bank and check your balance."

"Bank? What bank?"

"The best little bank on the island . . . Sterling Commonwealth."

With this a clap of thunder shook the building.


Her inflection was charming, but what she said was not.

"Your flight has been canceled due to inclement weather."

"It is very important that I get to the mainland as soon as possible," said Brad Axx.

Outside, what seemed like a hurricane was bending palm trees at a forty-five-degree angle.

The young woman stood before a computer terminal that had ceased functioning. "I wish there was something I could do for you."

"When is the next scheduled flight?"

"Four o'clock."

Today Birkett Gamble would be informed by First Gulf Bank via registered letter that his A-and-D application for fourteen million dollars had been denied. He was only going to get ten.

Tomorrow Birkett Gamble would protest the bank decision, although he'd agree with the terms so long as he could get the other four million in a few months if he behaved himself.

On Friday he would be on a bird out, following ten million A&D bucks plus one-point-eight million investor dollars that went south via EFT that morning.

"Is there a charter I could book?"

The attendant pointed to a yellow phone attached to a pillar. A sign above it said, NASSAU SHUTTLE. He went to it and lifted the receiver. He waited. After several minutes of this he hung up and he and Boomer went out front to a taxi.

"Nassau Shuttle," Axx ordered.

The driver muttered incoherently but drove off. Two minutes later they were in front of a hangar adjacent to the airfield. They sprinted toward a door marked OFFICE. Inside was nobody. They shouted. A man in a suit came out, obviously puzzled by their presence.

"We need a flight to Miami," said Axx.

The man began thumbing through papers. "I show no reservations for today."

"Not today," said Axx. "Now."

The office shuddered as another thunderclap sounded. "Now?" said the man. "You want to leave *now?*" He seemed delighted, as if by the senseless but charming notions of children.

"No spirit of adventure," said Boomer. "Come on, Brooklyn, we're going to do what everybody but you does when one of these hits—wait it out."

Everybody might have time to wait. Brad Axx did not.

$\triangledown$

# CHAPTER ELEVEN

THE door was flimsy and the lock presented no problem. Inside, the paraphernalia of persuasion still decked the walls: the aerial blowup of the site; photographs of happy residents enjoying the good life. In the dimness he almost walked into the floor model of River Woods. Under a plastic canopy, tiny people were frozen midstep. There were toy cars beneath midget palms, which provided shade from what would be the single reality of the scene—the barbecue-strength Florida sun.

Axx rummaged through files, looking for he was not sure what. Anything that could make a case against Birkett Gamble. He also wanted to know what Kristen had known. How deeply had she been into the scam?

If anything useful to him had been in the files, it was gone now. There had been plenty of time for a good job of culling by an interested party. But anxious people make errors, perhaps of oversight. Axx found none. It was getting dark. The late-afternoon flight from Nassau had departed on time, but he had still lost most of a day. He switched on a high-intensity desk lamp and resumed the search.

Finally he slammed the last file drawer shut.

Zip.

He checked a closet, found a cardboard box, which he opened. Inside were some of Kristen's personal belongings, including the beige walkabout shoes she wore the day they toured River Woods. There was also a Rolodex filer. He began going through it card by card. Kristen had been a real estate broker; there were a lot of cards. But one popped up reading like a neon sign: "New Era Construction," and below that several names, two of which were Bob Watts and Frank Garcia. He remembered them as Stick and Scarface, the construction workers Kritsen had questioned the day he had toured River Woods. Next to their names she had scrawled a question mark. He took the names down on a piece of paper, which he stashed in his wallet.

He swiveled in the chair, ready to leave the place.

An engine sounded outside, deep and gurgling. Axx turned off the light and waited. Two figures showed at the front door. When they entered, Axx switched on the desk lamp.

The girl yelped. It was Anne. Next to her was the cowboy from the Panhandle bar.

"My God, what are you doing here?" she gasped.

"Looking for answers."

The cowboy moved in front of her. 'I got one for you, dude." He reached behind his back and withdrew a knife in the Bowie family.

Axx stood. He smiled. Then he unholstered the .357. "Wrong answer."

"Son of a bitch!" The cowboy slammed the door shut behind him.

Axx lowered his weapon. "I was told Birkett canned you."

"I haven't finished cleaning out my desk."

"I hope that boy isn't stupid enough to come back carrying"

"He might be."

Axx started toward the door. He could feel the percussion before he heard it. Keeping low, he scuttled outside to see a 4×4 in flames.

Anne rushed past him. "Jason!" He caught her from behind and pulled her back into the office.

"They followed *you!*"

He had parked on the other side of the building among a cluster of pines. They had not seen him.

She began to shudder uncontrollably and he held her until she quieted. His eye caught a faint glow: Kristen's walking shoes. The canvas just above the soles was luminescent. He turned the overhead room light on for a better look, only to see the effect disappear. The sides of her shoes were still dusted by white powder. He switched off the ceiling light. The glow returned. He snapped off the desk lamp; in darkness, it was gone.

Whatever she had traipsed through was visible not in darkness or bright illumination but only in weak, indirect light.

To Anne he said, "You are going with me."

He took her to Boomer's for safekeeping. From behind the bar he grabbed a phone book. Under "Chemicals-Industrial," there were two listings, one for Gulf Shores.

Construction Chemicals Inc. was a warehouse with an attached front that served as office/salesroom. A sign in the door said, SORRY, WE'RE CLOSED. Axx turned the knob. It did not yield.

"Hold on!"

The lock was flipped and the door pulled opened by a weary-looking man in a short-sleeved shirt and brown tie. "What can I do for you?"

Axx lifted the pair of beige sneakers and pointed to the white stain.

The man adjusted his glasses. "I don't think they're my size."

"Turn the lights down."

"Beg pardon?"

"This white stuff on the sides, it shines. I need to know what it is."

The man took one shoe from Axx, examined it, sniffed it. "Phosphorus," he announced.

"You're sure?"

"I can smell the carbon."

"Who buys phosphorus?"

"Mostly contractors."

"What for?"

"Clearing underbrush. You put a match to this stuff and you've got yourself instant fire. It's safer than kerosene."

Axx had last seen this chemical in its unburned state at the side of a road near a rusty maroon pickup truck—the one belonging to Bob Watts and Frank Garcia of New Era Construction. But that area had already been cleared. Why lay a line of phosphorus in the dirt beside new blacktop? The workmen said they were inspecting the road for sewer drains, which would go in next.

Axx recounted all this to the manager, who said, "I heard the same damn story—what?—two weeks ago, maybe? This blonde was telling me the same damn thing. She had an idea what the stuff was. She wanted to know all about it."

"What did you tell her?"

"Just what I told you—I sell a lot of it, and don't wear good shoes when you use it or you won't be able to hide at night." He grinned. When Axx did not respond, he cleared his throat.

"Did you know her?"

"No. But her company does business with us."

"River Woods?"

"Right, but the account is with MFC." He went behind the counter and removed a thick looseleaf binder from a shelf under it. "They're one of our best customers. Last month . . ." His finger traced down several pages. He whistled. "Real good customer. I'm going to have to invite them to our picnic this year."

"Who at MFC orders phosphorus?"

"Nobody. The contractors order it when they need it. They just stop by and pick it up. We back-bill MFC."

"Any sales around the middle of April for River Woods?"

"Let's see. . . ." The finger did some walking. "Yep. Four fifty-pounders. No, that was the first. Here: the fourteenth, one lousy twenty-five-pound bag."

"Who ordered it?"

"That was . . . well, wait a minute. No contractor. Name of Ravitt. Walter Ravitt, with MFC."

"Who picked it up?"

"Hell, I don't remember that."

"Maybe two guys in a maroon pickup that had a hundred miles to live?"

The manager snapped his fingers. "You know, they wanted me to haul that bag to the truck for them. I said, I sell the stuff, brother. It's out back on a pallet by the fence if you want it. They didn't like that one bit." He shook his head.

"One of them wearing a scar along his face and neck?"

"That's the guy. The other was thin as a rail with hair down to his shoulders."

"Did they work for New Era Construction?"

"Nah, I know the New Era guys. These two I never seen before. But a couple weeks later, in they come again."

"Two weeks?"

"And they were here again today. Same guys, same truck, one twenty-five-pound bag."

"*Today?*"

"Take a look for yourself."

He swiveled the book about and there beside each order Axx saw the name Walter Ravitt.

Axx said, "Do you know Mr. Ravitt?"

"I know his signature. It's on the MFC checks I get for what they use at River Woods."

Axx said, "I'm trying to figure out why a guy who works in an office buys twenty-five pounds of phosphorus on the company tab."

"Nobody wants to pay for anything these days. Nobody wants to use their own money. These two guys probably dropped it off at his house and he used it to burn out some overgrowth in his backyard."

"He doesn't have one. He lives in a high rise."

"Well, maybe he gave it to a friend. There's plenty of that, too. Listen, I thought this sale was legit."

"No sweat."

The manager closed the book. "Police, huh?"

"Right." Axx picked up Kristen's shoes.

"Ever work in narcotics?"

"Yep."

"We get some sales there. 'Course, there's no way of telling. A sale is a sale."

"We are missing a piece here."

"The blonde, she didn't know either. I thought you said you did some narcotics work."

"New York City."

"Ahh." The manager nodded knowingly. "No good there. You need wide-open spaces."

"For what?"

"The drop. Look kind of funny, trying a stunt like that on Broadway. Probably kill somebody. Boom, right out of the sky." He chuckled. "Although from what I hear about that town . . ."

Axx placed the beige sneakers on the counter with deliberation.

"Hey," said the manager, "no offense intended."

It was just past midnight, but such were the hours Joseph Bono kept. He was a retired jailer from the Windy City. They found him working the graveyard shift in the communications room of the Wyatt County Police Department.

"Joe, I want you to meet Brad Axx," said Boomer. "He's down from New York."

"Please to meetcha. I like your town."

"You get there often?"

"Just once. Me and my partner had to stay over and bring back a prisoner the next day. Your people really gave us the royal treatment. First-class hotel, great food. They said if we wanted anything on the side, give them the word. We were a little backed up, you know how it gets. Our eyeballs were really floating. I am telling you, we left town the next day, our pipes were clean, brother."

"That's the way you left every town you ever went into," said Boomer.

"I loved to travel . . . minus the Mrs. Now here I be, filling in on the rotating shift for some swampy little PD in Florida when I am supposed to be home in bed so I can get up early and go sit on the beach. I got sick of the beach after one week, and if you gave me a golf club I wouldn't know which end was down."

"Why did you move to Florida?" Axx said.

"The Mrs. likes the sunshine. She hated every winter she ever spent in Chicago. Now it's my turn to pay while she plays." He turned to Boomer. "So, tell me. What does my old asshole buddy want from Joe Bono tonight?"

"A tap into your computer."

"You got it."

The man walked over to the terminal and flicked a switch. The machine began to hum, at which point he hit a key that brought to the screen: CODE:———.

He punched in a number and waited. What came up next was ENTER MODE, followed by LAST NAME:———, FIRST NAME:———.

From a piece of paper Axx read, "Watts, Robert." Bono typed this in, then hit the send button.

In a few minutes the computer at the Florida Crime Information Center in Tallahassee sent back this message: NO INFORMATION ON FILE, NO WATTS ON FILE.

"Nobody in this state knows the asshole," said Bono, "and nobody wants him."

"Punch up Garcia, Frank," said Axx.

Same response.

"Try an alias," said Axx.

Bono hit another key and on the screen appeared: SUBJECT HAS BEEN KNOWN TO USE FOLLOWING ALIASES:———.
He plugged in the name Bob Watts. Zero. Frank Garcia. Likewise.

"Sorry, pal," said Bono. "Looks like the cupboard is bare on these two."

"Can you spike into National from here?" said Axx.

"Sure."

More tap-tapping, more codes, and they were brain to brain with the National Computerized Criminal History System in D.C.

All of which produced two more negative hits.

"Alias again," said Axx.

To the entry, Watts, Robert, was reported: REAL NAME: WATERS, RONALD.

"Bingo," said Joe Bono. He tapped another key.

DOB: 5 FEBRUARY 1959.

APPROXIMATE WEIGHT: 130.

APPROXIMATE HEIGHT: 5'9".

COLOR EYES: BROWN.

COLOR HAIR: BLACK.

SCARS: NONE VISIBLE.

"Is that your man?" said Boomer.

"That sounds like Stick," said Axx.

The computer wasn't finished.

PAST HISTORY: POSSESSION OF STOLEN PROPERTY, 1979, LINCOLN NB, CONVICTED; DEALING IN STOLEN PROP-ERTY, OMAHA NB, 1984, DISMISSED; DRUG VIOLATION, 1985, DALLAS TX, DISMISSED.

"If you want more on this guy I can have them send his sheet," said Bono.

"This is all I need."

"Hold on," said Bono. He hit another key, which brought page two to the screen. SUBJECT KNOWN TO ASSO-CIATE WITH FOLLOWING PARTNER/PARTNERS: ESTEVEZ, FRANK.

Bono quickly punched up Estevez. The computer said: SUBJECT KNOWN TO USE FOLLOWING ALIASES: JUAREZ, TONY. GARCIA, FRANK.

"Nice work, Joe," said Boomer.

DOB: 14 JUNE 1955
APPROXIMATE WEIGHT: 180
APPROXIMATE HEIGHT: 5'10"
COLOR EYES: BROWN
COLOR HAIR: BROWN
SCARS: RIGHT SIDE FACE, NECK.
PAST HISTORY: ASSAULT AND BATTERY, 1974, BROWNS-VILLE TX, CONVICTED; GRAND THEFT AUTO, 1979, DAL-LAS TX, CONVICTED; DRUG VIOLATION, 1985, DALLAS TX, DISMISSED.

"That does it," said Axx.

"Looks like we owe you dinner some night, Joe," said Boomer.

"Better make it soon."

"Why?"

"I don't want to think about summer in this place. I am going north July One."

"What does the Mrs. say about that, Joe?"

"She can come along if she wants."

He tried to pick his way carefully but the sand spilled into his black wingtips. The sun was burning into the shoulders of his suit jacket, which he stripped off impatiently.

He looked up and down the beach and saw no one. Arlen was late again.

This was a deserted section of Pelican Key, not easily accessible, unattended by lifeguards, and so of little inter-est to tourists. He waited. It grew hotter. He had left his

sunglasses in the car. His eyes began to ache. He caught a
glint of white fabric near a stand of cedars back near the
road. In the shimmery brightness of midday it appeared to
be a mirage drifting toward him across a sea of sand. This
effect was enhanced by the snow white hair, now visible,
of a man several years younger than the comptroller.

"Christ, it's hot," Ravitt said annoyedly.

"You're dressed wrong," said the man. "In this line of
work, Walter, you must remain cool at all costs." He
spoke with a soft drawl. He was not a Floridian, but, like
Walter Ravitt, had been transplanted in a career move,
Ravitt was not sure from where. Alabama, maybe.

"You're late."

"There's time enough. You're always in such a rush,
Walter."

"I just like to see things happen when they're supposed
to happen."

"The . . . complication we discussed? That was resolved
to your satisfaction?"

"I would say that's old business."

"And is there any new business?"

"No."

"Everything is, as they say on the other coast, A-OK?"

"Yes. Listen, we have another five miles of road going
in if you want to increase the frequency."

"The schedule is biweekly, Walter, I would think that
would be clear by now."

"Sure. I just thought there might be—"

"If any adjustments are necessary, you will be notified.
Until then, we proceed as usual. Your people are prepared
for this evening?"

"Yes."

"I take it the last transaction was completed to every-
one's satisfaction?"

"Yes."

"Well, then, I would say we can now adjourn. I don't suppose we'll need to chat again soon, unless there is some other complication."

"Fine."

Ravitt shaded his eyes as he watched the man depart. Then he headed up the beach. He had a pounding headache. There were many rules for survival in Florida. He reminded himself again of this one: never, ever leave the sunglasses in the car.

When he got to the road, he saw a black sedan departing. He thought it was Arlen. But this car had two people in it. Arlen had brought a friend. This chilled him. He did not like Arlen's friends.

He should have gone back to the office. Instead he drove home. He was coaxing a cup of coffee from a batch of elderly grounds when the door to the bedroom opened. She came out in a short black thing that showed fleshy thighs. "You're home early."

"You slept all morning?"

"No. I had a buttered roll and watched TV and then went back to bed."

"You're the laziest woman I ever knew."

"You never knew another woman, Walter. Not like you know me. Besides, I like to conserve my energy." She crossed the room and subsided into the couch. "Did Lenore say anything?"

This was Birkett's secretary. He had told her Melanie was out sick again today. "She made a face and wrote something in your file."

"That bitch."

"Don't worry about it."

"When are you going to get me out of there?"

"Soon, Melanie, soon."

"That's what you keep saying but I don't get any action."

"These things take time."

"You keep saying that, too."

"I need you. You know that."

She jiggled a foot. "The super stopped by again today."

"What for?"

"He said he wanted to make sure it was okay."

The garbage disposal unit had malfunctioned a week earlier. Ravitt had not been able to get Burk to take a look at it until yesterday, Melanie's first day "out sick."

"He stopped by to do a quality control check, did he?"

"That's not why."

The way she said this brought a response that he wanted to deny but could not.

She said, "I told you what happened yesterday." Her eyes held his. "Do you want me to tell you about today?"

He swallowed hard. "Yes."

The phone rang. He thought it might be Arlen. Or Birkett. Perhaps Birkett had—

"Leave it," she said to him. She pulled herself up out of the couch. "Come on then. In the kitchen . . ."

Walter Ravitt's business career had entered uncharted waters and he was frightened but he would yield to the allure as he yielded to the distressing charms of this woman.

Because, like her, what he saw within reach was quite irresistible.

$\triangledown$

# CHAPTER TWELVE

He took the turnoff for the airport. He didn't go to the main terminal, instead continuing on to a collection of hangars. He stopped at one, which was open-ended and identified as the home of Saba Aviation. The car door opened and the white suit passed from sun into shade.

Axx pulled the black sedan around to the side. To Boomer he said, "Come looking if I'm not home by dark." He went to the mouth of the hangar. He saw no one but heard voices. He went inside, keeping to the perimeter. By a small plane he saw the man he was following with four others. Two of them looked familiar. He needed to get closer. He wanted to hear as well as see.

Just then the confab dispersed. The white suit headed back out. The men started toward Axx, who took cover behind a forklift. As they passed he recognized Curly and the Hulk, the pair who had manned the welcome wagon that night in the parking lot at Boomer's.

Axx sprinted outside. "He went thataway," said Boomer, pointing toward the main terminal. They caught up just as the other car turned into a rental dropoff lot. Axx followed. The man left the car and walked to a terminal passenger van.

"Looks like Whitey is leaving town," said Boomer.

Axx jumped out. "I'm with him unless he takes Sunshine Express."

"Watch your back, and I'll ask around about Wilbur Roos." Joe Bono's computer had turned up nothing on this man the previous night.

"Keep an eye on Anne."

"Not to worry, kid." Boomer swung the car toward Gulf Shores.

Whitey checked in, with a major carrier, for which Axx was grateful. At the counter, Axx identified himself and looked after the white suit heading toward the gates. "What flight is that gentleman taking?"

"Nine-oh-five to Tallahassee."

"What seat did you give him?"

"Twenty-four D, on the aisle."

"One way, on the aisle across from him, but a row back."

"How about two rows?"

"Sold."

On the way to the departure gate Axx passed an air courier office. He grabbed an envelope, then followed his man onto Flight 905.

Whitey had a drinking problem. He ordered doubles of Jack Daniel's. He amassed a platoon of tiny bottles that were swept away in preparation for arrival in Tallahassee. This event occurred with none of the dramatic flair of Axx's last entry into the capital. His man went directly to a waiting taxi. Axx expected to take the one next in line and follow. There was no line. There were no more taxis. So he hopped into the only one available.

"Hey!" said the driver.

"Double your money," said Axx. Then he turned to the man in the white suit. "Where you heading?"

"Downtown."

"Mind if I ride with you?" said Axx.

"I guess not."

Axx beamed at the driver. "Let's roll."

"I'm not supposed to do this."

Axx demonstrated the value of occasionally violating a rule for the right reason. The cabbie pocketed the bill and stepped on the gas. "Where to?"

"Oh, drop him off first," said Axx.

The driver looked in the rearview mirror. "Where's it gonna be?"

"HOB."

Axx grinned broadly. "Driver, you just won twice on the same horse. That's where I'm making my delivery." The other man looked at the air courier envelope in Axx's lap. "Rob Jameson," said Axx, extending his hand.

"Charmed."

Whitey looked out the window and Axx withdrew his unshaken hand, pleased that no more conversation would be forthcoming.

Soon they were deposited before a low building on the edge of the capitol complex. Axx kept just behind his man, slipping onto the same elevator. The man waited. Axx hit the button for three. The other man pressed four. At three, Axx stepped off and waited for the doors to close behind him. Then he sprinted for a sign that said, EXIT-STAIRWAY.

He took the steps two at a time, but when he arrived on four, Whitey was nowhere to be seen.

He started working the right side of the corridor, going in the first door. A large woman in a polka-dot dress sat at a desk facing him. A placard on the desk read "Sen. James Matthews." When she looked up Axx said, "That man in the white suit who just came in . . ."

She regarded him blankly. He left. He tried the next door. It was locked. So was the next. And the one after that. The following two were open. In one, nobody was home. In the next, he came upon another secretary, who was packing a cardboard box.

"The man in the white suit who—"

At the front of the desk was a nameplate engraved "Sen. Wilbur Roos."

"Mr. Ridgway?" said the secretary.

Axx just looked at her.

"Arlen Ridgway," she said. "He just arrived. Do you have an appointment?"

"He works for the senator?"

"Yes."

"I'd prefer to speak to Senator Roos."

"He's gone home. The session adjourned last week."

"Rats. When do they reconvene?"

"Next April."

Axx consulted his watch. "I'll have to come back."

A voice boomed out of a nearby office. "Irma, am I on with the senator?"

"Yes, at his home."

"In an hour?"

"Yes."

Axx immediately started out. The secretary said, "You'll still need an appointment, sir."

"Put me down for three o'clock on April the fifteenth."

The woman checked the only remaining item on her desk, a calendar. As the door closed she said, "The fifteenth is a *Sunday.*"

Axx decided if he were ever a rich man he would invest in an auto rental outfit. He was now parked in yet another car that did not belong to him at a curb near the House

Office Building. Many people went into and came out of this place; Arlen Ridgway was not among them.

A red convertible motored past. At the wheel was a man with white hair wearing a white jacket. Axx got the rental moving and fell in two cars behind.

The convertible left town and took a highway west. After thirty minutes it swung onto a two-lane road Axx was relieved to find congested. He kept at least one car between himself and Arlen Ridgway. When a single truck ahead of him turned off, Axx followed, then executed a quick three-point and got back on the road. This caused him to lose his quarry briefly, but he caught up. He followed at a greater distance.

They drove through a small town that resembled Gulf Shores in size but not style; by their storefronts, it was clear these shops were for the affluent. A mile beyond, Ridgway swung into a driveway leading to a gray stone house set back a hundred yards from the road. Out front was a sign on which was a wrought-iron likeness of a horse and the name ROOS.

Several cars and an RV were parked near the house. Axx headed back to town. He stopped at a restaurant and went to a phone. From the directory he got the listing for a local political organization.

To the voice that answered he said, "I admire Senator Wilbur Roos. I'd like to learn more about his political views."

"Wrong pew, pal."

*Click.*

Axx next found the number for the opposition party and repeated his request.

"Sure, where do I send it?"

"I'd like to stop by."

"We close up in fifteen minutes."

"I'm not far away."

"Where is that?"

Axx looked around. He put his hand over the mouthpiece as a waiter walked by. "Say, what do they call this joint?"

The waiter lifted his chin. "The name of this joint, sir, is Maison Gourmet."

"May your next tip be a big one, bubba."

Axx was only a block away. He walked it, arriving at a storefront displaying flags, stickers, and a large poster of The Man Himself. Inside were jammed several desks and a few file cabinets. A young man in a suit and tie sat at one of the desks. He looked tired, but he rose and greeted his visitor.

"Sorry to keep you," said Axx.

"No trouble. Always glad to talk to a Roos supporter."

"I'd like to know more about the senator."

"A fascinating man."

"I'm sure."

"An exceptional leader. He has a clear view of the realities of life, but he's a man of compassion as well."

"Do unto others. How long has he been in the Senate?"

"This is his third term. He has become a very prominent voice in the workings of that body."

"How so?"

The young man rattled off the senator's accomplishments, affiliations, and official responsibilities. ". . . and serves as liaison to the Air National Guard."

Axx perked up. "Is that a fact?"

"As you probably know, the Senate strongly supports the joint task force attempting to stem the devastating flow of drugs into our state."

"Tell me more."

"As part of this effort, the Air National Guard is using AWACs to spot small planes entering mainland airspace at night. They've been quite successful in identifying suspicious aircraft possibly carrying drug shipments. These planes are searched at the airport."

"And the senator has been working closely with the Guard in this program?"

"Oh, yes."

"How often do the AWACs go up?"

"I couldn't say for sure. The senator gave a talk to us last month on this and I think he mentioned they can't cover every mile of the state every night of the week, but each portion gets some coverage during any given week. Sometimes the planes are grounded altogether, for repairs, that sort of thing."

"The more I hear, the more I want to know about Senator Roos."

"I've been on staff here for three years and I think his future is unlimited. My guess is he'll run for governor in the next election."

"Really?"

"He has the ideas, the charisma, he would be able to do so many things if he occupied that office."

"It boggles the mind just to think about it."

"Of course, he's still considered a local politician. He's not widely known at the state level. But with this kind of man, any goal is within reach."

"Is he being asked to run?"

"Yes. And he has the people who can get the job done."

"Arlen Ridgway, for instance?"

"You know Arlen?"

"We shared a cab once."

"A take-charge guy. He could get a statewide campaign off the ground and really make it fly."

"Big campaigns cost big money."

"That would be the least of Wilbur Roos's worries."

"Well heeled, is he?"

"Independently wealthy."

"Any idea what he's worth?"

"Enough."

"Where did he make his money?"

"Investments, I understand. Real estate, stocks, metals . . ."

"A man like this, no telling what he's into."

"Unseating the incumbent won't be easy, of course. It never is. But this governor can be beaten, and Wilbur Roos is the man to do it." He folded his hands and contemplated the promising future of the state senator, and perhaps of those assisting him to greater office.

"I don't want to keep you any longer," said Axx.

"Shall I put you on our mailing list?"

"You'll hear from me. I am just getting started with Senator Roos."

The taxi cruised toward I-75.

It hadn't been easy, slipping away from her guardian, that Ellie something. Anne could hear the woman cursing as the taxi pulled away.

No way she was going to sit around some run-down shack of a hotel waiting for the people who had fire-bombed Jason's truck to find her.

She was leaving Gulf Shores for good.

The taxi passed over the interstate, then slowed as it turned onto a narrow unpaved road. She lived east of I-75, in an area yet undiscovered by real estate developers. The

sedan kicked up white dust as it approached a small frame
house set back among pines and palmettos.

"Right here is fine."

*"Here?"*

They were still fifty yards from her house. She paid him
and got out. He swung around and left her. Her nearest
neighbor was a quarter mile distant. This had been a
valued feature. Now she felt her isolation. She heard only
the low call of mourning doves and the raucous song of a
mockingbird.

The yard was empty but for her car.

All clear.

She would pack just one bag, and quickly. The destina-
tion was St. Louis, her hometown. She imagined herself
there, safe, with friends and family, alone no more. It
calmed her.

She looked at the balance in her checkbook: $654. She
had a five-thousand-dollar CD due in two months. That
could be handled by phone.

She thought she heard a metallic thud.

She stood for a moment there in the bedroom. The
interior was so familiar, so benign. She wished she did not
have to leave. She wanted to stay here until all of it—River
Woods, Birkett Gamble, that crazy policeman—all went
away.

Don't be a fool. Get your butt in gear, girl.

She grabbed the suitcase and barreled out the front door.
Just the other day, a silver Mercedes-Benz sat shining in
the sunlight.

She yanked open the door to her Honda. She wasn't
going in style, but she was definitely going.

★  ★  ★

"Is Mike in his office?"

"Yes. Who may I—"

"It's his brother."

"Just a minute, please." The man went to a corner office. At the door he said, "Your brother is here to see you."

"I'd like to meet him. I didn't know I had one."

The man reddened and started back to his post, but Axx was already past him. "Greetings, Mike! Not very brotherly of you."

The red-faced man said, "Shall I call security?"

"No, Ken," said the state attorney. "I remember him now. I just never liked him."

Ken was obviously a guy you could have a lot of fun with. He looked at Edwards and then Axx and then exited. Axx sat in one of two chairs before the state attorney's very large desk, at one corner of which was a glass-encased sign set in a silver base:

IF YOU'RE NOT PART OF THE SOLUTION,
GET THE HELL OUT OF THE WAY!

"Well, brother," said Edwards, "I still can't do a thing for you."

"You always could, you just never wanted to. But now I have something you want."

"And what is that?"

"Wilbur Roos."

A flicker of interest in the state attorney's eyes was not concealed.

"And why should I want Wilbur Roos?"

"Because he doesn't belong to your club. He's with the other boys. And he wants to be governor. You serve by the grace of the incumbent, so you surely *do* want Wilbur Roos."

"You think you can deliver him?"

"On your choice of platter—gold, silver, or platinum."

"And what do you want for him?"

"Birkett Gamble."

"All right," Edwards exhaled, "let's hear it."

"The second option payment Gamble made on River Woods, the two-seventy sent EFT from the numbered Nassau account? The account belongs to Roos on a DBA. The senator is laundering the green stuff he gets from bringing in the white stuff."

"What? Cocaine? Where did you get *that?*"

"It's coming into River Woods. At night."

"Boat?"

"The coast is hot, interdiction is doing some damage on the water. So it's by air. Phosphorus leads them in. The plane never touches down. The place is deserted. Nobody sees or hears anything."

"Have you got the bicycle?"

"Birkett is steering, his comptroller is pedaling. The wheels are some fly-boys at Saba Aviation and a couple of workers Birkett hired local. The workers are in the computer for drug arrests in Dallas in 1985."

"I don't see Wilbur Roos."

"The MFC comptroller is getting some help. From a Roos aide. Name of Arlen Ridgway." The state attorney's eyes widened. "The two gofers handle the logistics. Ridgway works out flight details, the MFC guy takes care of ground control."

"But the task force is using AWACs to spot incomings."

"Within a certain range during certain hours. That's what Roos brings to the deal. He is connected. He has official liaison with the Air National Guard. He can find out when to come in, and when to stay on the ground.

They can't lose—they don't risk offloading at the airport, and the AWAC isn't up when they do the fly-in. All they need is a nice, quiet site. River Woods is nine hundred acres with miles of new blacktop—easy in, easy out. It won't finish up for three years, maybe longer. At two drops a month, that's a lot of business."

"So with this sweet thing working for him, please tell me why Birkett Gamble wants to run a bust-out?"

"He's got marital problems. His creditors in Canada are looking for him down here. And he made a mistake. He killed somebody. The woman I told you about."

"The real estate broad? Why kill *her?*"

"She found out he was importing the stuff he was supplying her with. Maybe she wanted in on the action. That put me into it. The situation is getting a little out of control for Birkett Gamble. But he sees what he came down here for—a chance to walk away with at least ten big ones in his pocket . . . tomorrow."

"And on the basis of this flimsy supposition I am to exercise the considerable powers of my office and risk getting my ass in a very tight political crack?"

"I am talking to the DEA. If you don't want this, I have a feeling they will take it. Which means the governor has nothing to thank you for. In fact, when he finds out how you passed up a chance to do him a very large political favor . . ."

"How is he going to find out?"

"I will tell him."

"Mr. Axx, you certainly do know how to pitch a sale."

"I'm almost finished." Axx got to his feet and placed both hands on the big desk, leaning into his audience. Boomer would not approve, but Axx said it anyway. "I am going after Birkett Gamble no matter where in this world he thinks he is hiding. If that means punching a hole in your no-risk career, State Attorney Edwards, that is what I will do."

Axx lifted the glass sign from its supporting base on the corner of the desk. He placed it facedown in front of Michael Edwards.

"If you're not part of the solution, I will make you part of the problem."

The state attorney regarded Axx solemnly. Then he pressed a button on his telephone console.

"Yes sir?"

"You can come in now, Ken."

"She's gone," said Boomer. "Slipped away while we were at the airport."

Axx muttered a few indistinct expressions, then looked her up in the phone book.

She lived in a small frame house, in front of which was parked a red car, the door open. On the seat was a suitcase.

Her plan was good: get out of town. The problem was execution: don't pack, just get.

Axx turned to Boomer. "You fix that jeep yet?"

"Yep."

"We need it now."

They turned into River Woods and eased along the access road. The half-light of early evening was playing through the pines. They followed blacktop for two miles.

"There," said Axx.

Boomer pulled over. A hundred-yard strip of phosphorus ran along broken ground on each side of the road.

"They're coming in tonight," said Axx. "Birkett is going to pocket one last drop before he cuts and runs." In the distance he noticed a rickety-looking building. "What's that?"

"Well, it ain't a K-Mart, kid."

They advanced until Axx saw two things: a bridge and a truck. The bridge led to a small island, in the middle of which was a dilapidated ranch house. The truck was faded maroon and as beat up as the house.

"Get out of sight, fast like."

Boomer took the jeep straight for a clump of scrub palmetto. He had no sooner shut off the ignition than two men came out of the house. They hopped in the pickup and clattered over the bridge. Axx and Boomer drew their weapons. The truck passed on.

"Know them?" said Boomer.

"Stick and Scarface, the two guys we punched up on the computer. They work for Birkett. I want to get into that house."

"I figured you would."

They approached by foot. On the front door was a brand-new padlock. They went around to a window, through which they saw one room.

No Anne.

Boomer jimmied the window. The furnishings were spare: six Formica tables of considerable vintage and assorted hard-backed chairs. The tables were arranged in a horseshoe shape around a 140-kilowatt portable generator. This was hooked up to an industrial-size dough mixer.

"It's a bakery," said Boomer, "but the dough boy isn't here yet."

"He will be tonight."

Lined up across five of the tables were shallow sheet-pans. Each had a piece of tape bearing a notation: F6, B11, R32.

"Codes identifying the route men," aid Axx.

On the sixth table was a set of scales, along with a stack of plastic bags and rolls of tape. The contents of the pans would be bagged and shipped to different locations for further distribution.

They climbed out the window and went to the rear of the ranch house. Tied up at a dock were two sleek thirty-foot racers fitted with twin two-hundred-horsepower outboards.

"After they cut it, they pack it in waterproof bags and take it out by boat," said Axx. "Why would they do that? The Gulf is full of heat."

"They're not going into the Gulf. They're heading upriver. Nobody on the river is looking for them. Must be a hundred spots they could offload to a car or truck."

"We have to hit them here."

"I missed that. My hearing aid wasn't turned up."

"The state attorney thinks I'm talking to the DEA. I'm not."

"You bring a howitzer down from New York with you?"

"If I was back home, I'd use something better—a mini-TOE."

"Mini-which?"

"Ton-of-explosives rocket launcher. Fits in a suitcase."

"I'll check the Samsonite but I don't think I have one."

"We'll need help."

"I heard *that*. Incidentally, it gets dark in two hours. Out here, it gets very dark."

"Then we'll have to get help in a hurry."

"Just who do you have in mind?"

When they arrived at the aging stone structure that was the municipal building/police headquarters, Chief Leroy Snow was locking his desk.

"Hiya, Chief," said Axx.

"Don't sit down unless you want to stay until I open up in the morning."

Boomer said, "Your day is just beginning."

"I'm late for dinner."

"We'll order out," said Axx. "But myself, I don't like to do this kind of work on a full stomach."

"What kind of work is that?"

"Apprehension and arrest, Chief," said Boomer. "You are going to catch some drug smugglers in the act. And if we guess right, you will also come to the rescue of a young damsel in great distress. You are going to be a very newsworthy personality in Florida law enforcement."

Axx laid it out for him. The chief eased his bulk into a chair that shrieked in protest. As he listened he was in turn amazed, angered, and finally outraged: an operation like this was being run in his territory and nobody had even *attempted* to take care of him.

This, of course, was what his visitors were counting on.

"Well, what do you think, Chief?" said Axx.

"I think we have a problem."

"Chief, if you do not cooperate—"

"I'm talking tactics, boy." He unrolled the kind of map sold in marinas and leaned forward in the raucous chair. He pointed to the island where the ranch house was located. "Getting across that bridge is like being a duck on opening day. And while we shoot our way in the front, they go out the back."

"No problem," said Axx. "We send somebody in by boat."

"Ain't got no money for no speedboat. You said they
have two?" Axx nodded. "They load the dope in one,"
Snow continued. "The other is escort—and it'll be waiting
right *here*. . . ." He indicated a sliver of land where the
canal leading out from behind the ranch house met the
river beyond.

"So we borrow a boat," said Axx.

"Channel be narrow back in there. You'd have to slow
up in that dark. Boys in the escort would have to try hard
to miss you." He studied the map. "What we need here is
your element of surprise." A stubby finger thumped down
on the map. "They won't be looking *this* way."

Boomer leaned over his shoulder. "They sure won't.
That's all marsh, is why. Can't be but a foot deep, even
less if the tide is out. How you plan on getting across?"

"Buggy."

Axx stood in a garage that was bigger than the house next
to it.

"Used to be a barn," said Bubbles, its owner. Bubbles
was first cousin to the Gulf Shores chief of police. "I need
the space for my machines."

These were black and gleaming below the undiluted
wattage of many unshaded bulbs strung on wires across
the garage. Airbrushed in orange were their names: *Big
Ripper* and *Loose Goose*. They looked like airplanes without wings. Except for the wheels, of course. The rear tires
of *Big Ripper* were shoulder high. The treads were three
inches deep.

"Deep-cleat tractor tires," said Bubbles, "for rice and
sugar fields, where it's real sloppy. I cut them a little
deeper for more grab. Now these up here"—the front
wheels were fitted with what looked like oversized bicycle

tires—"they were one dog who was hard to find. Bought 'em used off a celery and cabbage farm, where they got them skinny rows to tractor."

The unmatched wheels supported a molded fiberglass body nineteen feet long, at the rear of which sat an eight-cylinder thousand-horsepower engine. "Brand new Chevy block, stroked and bored up to six hundred and five cubic inches."

"Swamp buggy!" said Leroy Snow happily. "Run through a foot of water or five feet, don't matter. Just what we need *tonight!*"

Bubbles was fingering one of several decals that identified contributors helping finance this machine—Thompson Tobacco, Schwinn Septic, Westside Pump . . . not your run-of-the-mill Indy 500 sponsors, but benefactors nonetheless.

"Whaddya mean *tonight?*" Bubbles said. "Can't they wait until morning?"

The chief draped an arm about the broad shoulders of his first cousin. "I lied, Bubbles. They don't want to back *Big Ripper*. They want to use it. To bust some drug boys out at River Ranch. And I want that one." He nodded at the slightly smaller companion model, *Loose Goose*.

Bubbles removed the arm from his shoulder. "No, Leroy! I say no and I mean *no!* Are you crazy, boy? Get my buggies all shot up and maybe wrecked? You know how much they *cost?*" When Leroy paid no attention to this, Bubbles said, "Twenty thousand, Leroy! *Twenty* . . . each!"

"Bubbles, how much money would you bring home if you won one of those trophies down in Naples?"

"A thousand, fifteen hundred maybe."

"How many times a year they race down there?"

"Twice. But they say they're gonna expand."

"How long you been racing?"

"I don't know."

"Seven years. How many races you won, Bubbles?"

"Three or four."

"Not heats. Finals."

Bubbles shoved his hands deep into his coveralls. "Nobody much beats those Naples boys, but I will one of these days. Besides, that's all the more reason to keep my buggies in one piece. I need to protect my investment, Leroy."

"Say there, Mr. Axx, how much you figure the state ought to reimburse my cousin here for the use of his private property in this o-fficial capacity?"

"At least two thousand."

Bubbles perked up. "And who pays me that, you?"

"The state attorney. His budget is unlimited. I'd recommend twenty-five hundred."

"Apiece."

Axx nodded.

"Plus repairs."

"Only fair."

Bubbles clapped his hands.

The chief said, "We need one more machine. Where's the wife's?"

"In the carport. I'll fetch the key." He turned to a small boy who had been listening, goggle-eyed. "Go tell your mama we need her buggy."

"She won't like that a'tall."

Bubbles raised his hand and the boy raised dust. "Annie races the jeep," he explained to Axx.

The chief said, "Deputy Warren here will take the jeep with Mr. Boomer. You and me, cousin, go in with *Loose*

*Goose*. Mr. Axx . . ." The chief patted the exterior of *Big Ripper*.

The windows of the ranch house glowed three hundred yards distant. Axx sat high in the cockpit listening to last-minute instructions from Bubbles. The Colt rested against his rib cage. He wore a zip-up jacket that was supposed to keep it dry.

"Downshift when you hit a hole," said Bubbles. "You're gonna have to push water to get out."

"Hole? I thought it was just a foot deep out there."

"Mostly. When you get clear, go into high gear and haul ass."

"What will she do?"

"Sixty in shallow." He grinned toothily. "A lot less in a hole. And don't be 'fraid to lean on that gearshift, this ain't no BMW."

"What happens if the engine gets a bath?"

"That's what buggy racing is all about. Don't worry, *Big Ripper* always finishes."

Axx checked his watch, which he now realized was not waterproof: midnight. He turned the ignition key. The engine seemed to explode.

Bubbles leaned close to his ear. "We fer-git the muffler!" Then he hopped down and climbed into *Loose Goose*.

A flare went up beyond the island. This was the signal from the deputies storming the bridge.

"Let's *go!*" Leroy Snow bellowed.

Axx let one thousand horses loose. In an instant he was blasting across marsh, the buggy dipping and diving. Water gushed past, over, and into the cockpit. He wiped mud from his eyes. Halfway across he hit a hole. He downshifted, pushed in deeper, deeper still. Water washed about his waist. The engine stalled, the monstrous roar dying away.

Bubbles went flying by in *Loose Goose.* Axx had identified the hole.

He eased up on the accelerator, stomped down. The engine caught and the swamp buggy shot up and out. Now he was flying again, the island coming up fast. He saw two men run out of the house. Light spilled from a doorway. They each carried a large plastic bag, which they tossed into a boat at the dock. They looked out at the marsh. They could not see what was coming, but they could hear it.

One of them ran back into the house. The other moved out of the light onto an embankment. Moonlight glinted off the barrel of a rifle as it was raised.

A bullet punctured the cockpit of *Big Ripper,* then another. The gunman was straight ahead but Axx could not stop or he would be a sitting target. He held steady and hoped he did not find another hole. The buggy hit the shoreline wide open. The gunman was propelled up and over, arms and legs askew, like a rag toy.

Axx braked as the second man came out of the ranch house and lifted a revolver. It was Stick. Axx's .357 was already leveled. The impact blew the man back through the doorway. Axx clambered out and down. Nearby, motionless, was Scarface.

Bubbles skidded the *Loose Goose* ashore as Axx sprinted toward the door. Snow fell in behind. From the canal Axx heard shots. The escort boat was rocketing in, drawing fire from the jeep. The escort hit the dock at full speed. End of boat and dock.

Axx and Snow shouldered through the back door as the deputies came stomping in the front. Two men Axx did not recognize stood with their hands raised.

Snow said, "Lock 'em down." The deputies yanked handcuffs loose.

In a corner lay Annie Johns, tied and gagged.

A deputy began cutting her loose. Axx hustled back outside. The jeep was climbing onto the island. Boomer gave him the thumbs-up. The dock was in flames, by the light of which he could see the driver of *Loose Goose* sitting stone-faced in the cockpit.

The chief came out and sauntered over to his first cousin, who said, "Can please we go *home* now, Leroy?"

A banner strung above the dais trumpeted a familiar refrain: RIVER WOODS . . . A COMMUNITY IN NATURE. WE'RE ON OUR WAY!

About one quarter of the 177 living, breathing River Woods investors were on hand for a continental breakfast at the Airport Royale, a stone's throw from Kingston terminal. They were just biting into their danish when someone began rapping on a half-empty water glass. All heads lifted. Birkett Gamble slowly got to his feet. He leaned into the microphone, which was not necessary in order for him to be heard but which he thought was the right touch.

"Welcome. This is a great day, the day we have long worked for, prayed for, the day we break ground for your new home—River Woods!"

This was uttered with an evangelical crescendo that rose in pitch and was accompanied by applause.

"The fine people at First Gulf Bank have this very morning given us the initial funding that will help make our dream . . . *come true!*"

Loud applause.

Among those admiring this performance were two men not seated at tables. They stood out of sight, stage right.

"He's a good one," said Michael Edwards.

Brad Axx listened to Birkett Gamble with contempt and fascination in unequal measure.

The speaker told of his own dream, which he had brought with him from a distant, different place, a country that did not cherish the fragile framework of the free enterprise system, by which those willing to take risks and make sacrifices can build a better life for themselves and their families.

The state attorney was restless. He whispered something to an agent of the Florida Department of Law Enforcement. He unzipped a black leather case. From this he removed a copy of the court order freezing all assets of MFC Inc. This had already negated Birkett's instructions to First Gulf that the ten million A-and-D dollars deposited first thing that morning in the MFC account be transferred immediately to Banco Nacional, Republic of Panama—along with approximately one-point-eight million dollars received from River Woods investors, many of whom were now listening raptly.

"We will be communicating with all of you in the near future as to how construction is proceeding," the speaker concluded. "I know you are all anxious to begin your new lives in your new homes. For now, thank you. And remember, he who no longer dreams . . . no longer lives!"

Birkett Gamble waved and started out. The audience stood in acclaim.

He was met halfway by Michael Edwards, who identified himself and stated his business.

Gamble glanced beyond at Brad Axx, then asked Edwards, "May I ask for what reason I am being arrested?"

"Mail fraud . . . conspiracy to defraud . . . racketeering associated with the promotion of the River Woods development project . . . murder, in the death of Kristen McCauley . . ."

"That is ridiculous, I had nothing to do—"

". . . importation of an illegal substance . . . conspiracy to distribute an illegal substance . . . trafficking in an illegal substance. Mr. Metcalf—"

There was a metallic rattle. The audience, silent now, remained motionless as the FDLE agent snapped on the handcuffs.

"Illegal substance?" said Gamble. "*What* illegal substance?"

"Your drop operation at River Woods was hit last night," said Edwards. "We picked up the whole crew, along with a very important person the federal people have been interested in locating for several years."

"Will you tell me what in the hell you are talking about? What drops? What crew? At River Woods, you say?"

The state attorney affected the weary attitude of one who must explain the obvious. "You made a boo-boo, Mr. Gamble. You let the money show. The two-seventy laundered through Nassau? It was traced back to Senator Roos."

"Laundered?"

"Okay, let's get him out of here."

"Listen, I am telling you I know *nothing* about any drug operation. That half-wit son of a bitch Roos! That—"

Gamble was nudged ahead by the FDLE man, who led him past Brad Axx toward a side door.

"Well, congratulations," said Michael Edwards. "He came down from Canada and you made like the Mounties."

Axx should have felt triumphant. He did not. When he

understood why, he said, "What time is it?" He no longer owned a wristwatch that worked.

"Nine-forty," answered the state attorney, who then watched as Brad Axx tried to get to the front door by knocking aside as few River Woods investors as possible.

▽

# CHAPTER THIRTEEN

His man stood between two suitcases.

Brad Axx would bet the contents of both that neither had Walter Ravitt's jammies in them.

"Island hopping, Walter?"

These words were nearly lost in the cavernous confines of Saba Aviation. But they were heard. Ravitt nearly tripped over his luggage getting himself turned around. "Axx . . ."

"Ask me what I'm doing here."

"Why, you found me out, of course. You arrested Birkett and he didn't know a thing about any drug drops and you knew he was telling the truth."

"Which left guess who."

"When I didn't get a call from Ronnie last night, I knew I was in trouble sooner or later. I was hoping it would be later."

"It is right now, Walter."

Axx checked him for concealed. "Not my style," said Ravitt.

"Birkett's words when I told him he killed Kristen. But she met *you* after she left Birkett's boat that night. You were her supplier."

Ravitt shrugged. "She had weaknesses. One of them wasn't me or I wouldn't have spent thirty seconds with that little tramp at the office. But she was smart, Kristen. She figured out what we were doing at River Woods . . . the phosphorus, the new locks on the ranch house, how I had such good stuff I could give her. It would have been better for her if she understood what Birkett was after. But none of us did."

"She didn't know about the bust-out?"

"Only the false certificates. She tried to cut herself a deal with Birkett."

"What kind of deal?"

"She wanted full commissions, no more fifty-fifty split."

"Why should he go for that?"

"She figured because he stood to make big bucks on River Woods, he'd give on the commissions if she threatened to expose the certificate thing."

"But she would have gone down in flames with him."

"She was a very grasping woman, lovely Kristen. She wanted as much as she could get. As it turned out, she was bargaining for one hundred percent of nothing. Birkett was getting ready to check out. She hadn't a clue to that, of course. None of us did."

"So it wasn't a piece of Birkett's bust-out she wanted," Axx said. "She wanted in on your end. In case Birkett threw her overboard."

"I agreed, of course."

"Then you fed her poison. Where?"

"By the beach. She always picked up from me there. I told one of the boys to wait a couple hours, then take her home in her own car. Kristen . . . wasn't something I wanted to do. It was something I had to do."

"Sure. Makes sense. If Kristen is history, you can't lose. Birkett is happy. He lucked out—she overdosed doing drugs. But now I'm on the case, screwing up his bust-out."

"You were a gift."

"How did you know I was a cop?"

"Kristen. She tried to use her New York narc to put the screws to me. She reasoned the locals were taken care of. Or would be. But Arlen was greedy, he didn't want to share unless he had to."

"Was Anne in this with Kristen?"

"Annie idolized Kristen. Kristen used the mushroom method—keep her in the dark and feed her shit. Or so I thought. But Annie found out a few things. I was doing the paperwork on the phony certificates for Birkett, and he said Annie knew what we were doing and was pushing him. I figured maybe she knew about the fly-ins, too. She had to go."

"How long did you figure you could keep the drops going after Birkett's bust-out was blown?"

"Six months at least, maybe a year. I was fairly clean on River Woods. Birkett was president and treasurer. I'd cooperate with the investigation, testify against him. That way I'd get to stay around until the courts worked it out and the bank took over."

"What was your cut of that?"

"A hundred per drop, two drops a month."

Axx kicked over a suitcase, which thumped heavily. "How much?"

"One fifty. It's for the pilot. I kept it handy just in case. The rest was direct deposit by Arlen. Sterling Commonwealth, of course. Birkett isn't the only guy in town with a secret bank account."

"You should have left this town a long ago time ago."

"Walk away from a money machine? That white powder, people become *billionaires* in this business!"

"They also become dead. Or convicts. Which is what I have in mind for you, Walter."

He caught movement from the side. He dropped to one knee as a bullet went past his head. Axx fired and the gunman spun about, his weapon twisting in an arc, then dropping beside him in the dirt. Axx went over. It was Curly.

Axx glanced about, saw no one else. But the vicinity would soon become crowded.

"Pick up those bags and move," Axx said to Ravitt. "You already know Leroy Snow. I want to introduce you to the state attorney."

Ravitt's eyes grew large. Too late Axx realized it was not in fear.

He did not hear Walter Ravitt say, "What the hell kept you?"

When he regained a portion of his senses, Brad Axx was lying on a hard surface in the dark. He thought he heard water running. He definitely heard conversation.

"Why can't we just dump him out over the ocean?"

"This ain't no drop from the Piper, Mr. Ravitt. It's gonna be a Learjet with a pressurized cabin. It's gotta stay pressurized. Which means we don't send this boy skydiving without no parachute."

"So why can't we use the Piper?"

"Because the Piper ain't ready."

"Are you sure this is going to work?"

"If they find him, all is left is bone. He's gator meat."
The man grunted. Something heavey fell onto something

wooden, which was the dock where Axx lay. "Come over here and give me a hand."

Axx opened one eye. Beside him was what in Brooklyn was known as a cinder block. Next to this was a coil of rope that looked strong enough to tie up a cruise ship. At the rear gate of a maroon pickup were Walter Ravitt and a second man, who was enormous. It was the Hulk, who now had a fine opportunity to repay Axx for a shattered face. They began hauling more blocks onto the dock.

Axx had an idea the rope, the cement blocks, and himself all would be of a piece very soon.

His revolver was no longer on his person. A twin-trigger shotgun leaned against the pickup.

He tried to consider his options but the computer was not yet fully on line. Pain overloaded his brain. It was centered in that portion of his anatomy where his shoulder met his neck. Somebody had tried to cleave the two, probably with the barrel of that shotgun.

"Shouldn't we tie him up here?" said Ravitt.

"This is a public ramp. No telling when some old boys out night fishing might come in. It's safer on the water."

Axx decided it was time to get into gear. He tried.

"Hey, he's moving."

"Take this and watch him until I finish."

A kick was delivered into Axx's ribs. "Relax," said Ravitt. "It's not time yet."

Axx eased himself up until he sat with his back against a piling. His vision cleared. What he saw was his own gun pointed at him.

"So poor Birkett stays and little Walter flies."

Walter Ravitt smiled smugly. "Birkett thought he'd be in Panama by now."

"Birkett opening up the numbered account there must have been a real shocker."

Ravitt gripped the gun tighter. "I couldn't let the bastard do it. It was me who introduced him to Wilbur Roos.
I went to school with Teddy Roos. I was best man at his
wedding. He was always telling me how they were getting
rich in real estate, how I went into the wrong work."

"But you were doing Janice Kern's taxes. You met the
new hubby. He had big ideas about real estate."

"Birkett was full of ideas. What he didn't have was cash.
He needed two hundred and seventy thousand for the
second option payment. His wife wasn't going to give it
to him."

"Wilbur Roos had it."

"He told Birkett he might be able to do him a few
favors, on the political end. So he wanted his investment
kept quiet. But he needed somebody on the inside looking
after his interests."

"Which was you."

"There's not much money in crunching other people's
numbers, Axx. Not nearly enough."

"So you got to be an officer."

"I demanded that. Birkett didn't much like the idea, but
Roos said, let's make it official. Personally I wanted cre-
dentials for after River Woods built out. I was going to
stay in real estate."

"Then you saw the senator's two-seventy come in from
Nassau."

"I couldn't believe it. I thought the guy was legitimate.
So did Birkett."

"What did you do?"

"I didn't tell Birkett. All he knew, the money was in. I
was interfacing with Arlen, who ran everything for Roos.
When I queried Arlen about the source of the good senator's funds, he didn't even try to play dumb. He came
right out with it."

"He also said they needed a new way to bring in the white stuff."

"Arlen saw River Woods as perfect. It was."

"So when I got to be a problem, you didn't talk to Birkett, you called Arlen."

"He said he'd take care of it."

"But you were supposed to look after their interests, Walter. You knew Birkett was playing games . . . the sales numbers, the certificates."

The Hulk loaded the last of the cinder blocks into the boat.

Ravitt said, "Birkett would have gotten away with the certificate thing. Too many people wanted River Woods to succeed. But I couldn't understand why he was doing it. He could postpone the A-and-D until he had the right numbers."

"He couldn't wait. His Toronto creditors were ready to go to court down here, his wife was after him, he had to take the money and run."

"I see." Ravitt shifted his grip on the .357.

Axx wondered if the man had ever held a handgun before, and if the damn thing was going to go off accidentally with Brad Axx in front of it. "How did you find out about Birkett's Panama account?"

"He used the company name, so it would be a simple transfer of corporate funds. Some nit at First Gulf decided I should be kept informed. The bastard was going to leave me holding the bag."

"There was no way you could tell Arlen about that, was there? By then it was too late."

"I was the guy who hooked them up with Birkett. I saw how they went after you." Work boots thudded along the dock; the big man carried the corpse of Curly to the boat. "After they finished with Birkett, they'd look for me. They'd figure I was part of it from the beginning—the bad numbers, the phony certificates. It would look like I just chickened out. They wouldn't listen to a word I said."

"But if I nailed Birkett, that might fix things for you."

"You'd prove I knew nothing about Birkett's big scam. I'd be clear with Arlen. And I figured if you were going after Birkett Gamble, you'd be going away from Wilbur Roos. I could keep our important enterprise going."

"But I found what you found, Walter—the Nassau account Roos was using to launder."

"You were good, Axx. Excellent, in fact." The other man returned with the shotgun. "However, I'm afraid you lose."

The Hulk took the .357 from Ravitt and tossed it in the river. "Start the boat," he said. "Make some noise."

Axx pushed hard off the piling, driving with his legs. For his trouble he took the butt of the shotgun across his face.

There followed the gutteral grunt of an outboard motor. It began to rev up. Axx got to his hands and knees. Against his temple he felt the cool barrel of the shotgun, along the length of which was transmitted the cocking of a trigger.

There were two quick shots and Axx rolled away. The big man staggered, let loose a blast that tore a jagged hole in the dock, and fell.

Walter Ravitt cast off lines in a panic. He stumbled toward the controls, and the boat surged forward.

Axx tossed the .25 Browning aside. Once again it had been overlooked. Once again it had saved him.

He lifted the shotgun and cocked the second trigger. The boat was racing toward open water. Axx fired. The load blew away much of the transom and some of Walter Ravitt, who let go of the wheel and grabbed at his leg. The speedboat veered crazily ahead, engine sputtering. Axx had no more shells. The boat disappeared into the darkness of the river. He could not hear the engine.

He sat on the edge of the dock and began to massage his neck. This was supposed to ease the pain, which sharpened. A better idea would be to get in the truck and drive away from here. He was at the wheel when he heard the shouts.

"My God, no! Somebody help me! Somebody *please* help me!"

There followed a single scream, which ended abruptly.

Axx had no way of knowing that Walter Ravitt had finally found some luck. He would die by drowning.

On the other hand, there would be no plea bargain for manslaughter two.

$\triangledown$

# CHAPTER FOURTEEN

A BLACKENED amberjack sandwich wrapped in tin foil was on the seat beside him. In his pocket was a ticket for Flight 412 departing Kingston FL for LaGuardia NY via Atlanta GA in two hours. He would drop off the rental and be up, up, and away.

Ellie came around the driver's side of the car and gripped his neck in a fierce hug. "You take care of yourself, hear?"

Anne Johns leaned in and gave him a quick kiss. "What are your plans?" he said.

"Work here for a while, then maybe get into residential resales again. A lot can happen to you, but it doesn't usually include bombs and bullets."

The proprietor of Boomer's shoved a big hand at him. "Keep your knees loose, Brooklyn—"

"—and your glove oiled, Pop."

He stepped on the accelerator, pulling away from the weathered facade of the big white house. The figures in the sun-lit roadway receded in the rearview mirror.

Soon he was bursting up I-75. He was not sure why he was trying to make time when he had two hours for a forty-five-minute drive. It dawned on him when he found himself turning right instead of left at Kingston.

Fittingly the cemetery had been cut out of what had been a ranch. He knelt beneath the burning sun before her grave, which was marked by a stone set in the sandy soil.

He ran his fingers along the rough surface of the gravestone. Her skin had been so silken.

No, for this case the old mind trick had not worked.

It never did.

If you have enjoyed this book and would like to receive details of other Walker Mystery-Suspense novels, please write for your free suscription to:

*Crime After Crime Newsletter*
Walker and Company
720 Fifth Avenue
New York NY 10010